Hamsters Need Help

Hamster in a Hamper

Illustrations by Shelagh McNicholas

Hamster in the Holly

Illustrations by Jenny Gregory

LUCY DANIELS

d-up edition published in 2   ed's Books

Special thanks to Jenny Oldfield.
Thanks also to C. J. Hall, B.Vet.Med., M.R.C.V.S., for reviewing
the veterinary information contained in this book.

Hamster in a Hamper
Text copyright © 1996 Working Partners Limited
Illustrations copyright © 1996 Shelagh McNicholas
First published as a single volume in Great Britain in 1996 by Hodder Children's Books

Hamster in the Holly
Text copyright © 1998 Working Partners Limited
Illustrations copyright © 1998 Jenny Gregory
First published as a single volume in Great Britain in 1998 by Hodder Children's Books

Animal Ark is a trademark of Working Partners Limited
Created by Working Partners Limited, London WC1X 9HH
Original series created by Ben M. Baglio

The right of Lucy Daniels to be identified as the Author of the work has been asserted
by her in accordance with the Copyright, Designs and Patents Act 1988.

1

A Catalogue record for this book is available from the British Library

ISBN 978 1 444 90730 8

Typeset in Baskerville by Avon DataSet Ltd,
Bidford-on-Avon, Warwickshire

Printed and bound by CPI Group (UK) Ltd, Croydon, CR0 4YY

The paper and board used in this paperback by Hodder Children's
Books are natural recyclable products made from wood grown in
sustainable forests. The manufacturing processes conform to the
environmental regulations of the country of origin.

Hodder Children's Books
a division of Hachette Children's Books
338 Euston Road, London NW1 3BH
An Hachette UK company
www.hachette.co.uk

Hamster
in a
Hamper

One

Mandy Hope sat with her chin cupped in both hands. She was daydreaming in class, while sun streamed in through the biology lab window. Miss Temple was handing back the homework books. Mandy gazed at Henry the Eighth, the school hamster, treading steadily inside his exercise wheel.

Henry the Eighth was a good name, she decided. Like all hamsters, Henry had a funny habit of pouching his food in his cheeks, which puffed out, making him look enormously fat and self-important. His golden brown whiskers and the flash of white on the chest completed his resemblance to the famous king of England.

Treadle-treadle-rattle-spin went the wheel. Henry's squat little legs trotted on. Mandy smiled absent-mindedly. Henry was the eighth and last hamster in his litter, hence his name. Miss Temple had found homes for all the rest, but had decided to keep Henry as the school pet. She said he was a hamster with attitude. Mandy supposed this meant that he had a cheeky glint in his enormous dark eyes. Anyway, Henry had turned into one of the friendliest little animals, happy to sit in your hand nibbling dry porridge oats or to take a small chunk of brown bread and hold it delicately between his front paws.

And that was the problem; he was too friendly and too greedy. Everyone who came up to his cage for a chat slipped him a few goodies. He gobbled crisps, sandwich crusts, apple cores. You name it, Henry ate it. And he was fat!

He had a nice life though, sitting inside his airy wooden cage on the sunniest ledge in the biology lab, alongside the geraniums and the spider plants. He'd put on weight, and no amount of treading the exercise wheel seemed to take it off again. Podgy, pouchy, overweight little Henry weighed in at a mighty one hundred and fifty grammes. He was a heavyweight hamster. Mandy smiled and dreamed on.

'Mandy Hope.' Miss Temple's voice brought her back to earth. 'Hello, Mandy. Knock, knock, is anybody there?' She came up to Mandy's bench and rattled her knuckles against it, exercise book at the ready. 'Don't you want to know your homework grade?'

Mandy blushed and pushed her blonde hair behind her ears. 'Sorry.' Sheepishly she took her book.

'Don't worry. Only one more day to go before we break up!' Miss Temple's smile was warm and friendly. 'You're not the only one who can't wait for the end of term.'

This time Mandy grinned. She liked the biology teacher, and this wasn't just because biology was her favourite school subject, with all the fascinating facts about animals. Miss Temple herself was bright and young; quite strict when she wanted her pupils to pay attention, but open to a joke and a kind word. She didn't look like a teacher either, with her wavy brown hair straying out of its ponytail and her light summer dresses.

'I was watching Henry doing his workout,' Mandy explained.

Miss Temple glanced at her watch and told the class to pack away their things. 'Ah, our dear little

Mesocricetus auratus! That's his official, scientific name.' She smiled, glancing at Henry. 'Or not so little, as the case may be. He could really do with being put on a strict diet. And that reminds me.' She walked back to the front of the class and clapped her hands for attention. 'Listen for a moment, everyone!'

Mandy watched a couple of people in the front row having a whisper and a giggle behind their hands. End-of-term fever was really setting in. One girl, Vicki Simpson, had gone bright red and sat on the edge of her seat. She watched Miss Temple step up the ledge towards her own demonstration bench. Vicki's friend, Becky Severn, dug her in the ribs and warned her to be quiet. Meanwhile, Vicki's twin brother, Justin, retreated from Miss Temple's bench, a wide grin spread across his round, freckled face.

Miss Temple clapped again and the room fell silent. 'I want to make an announcement before the bell goes.' She paused and cocked her head to one side. She listened hard. 'What's that noise?'

In the silence, Mandy could hear Henry plodding steadily inside his wheel. *Treadle-treadle-rattle-spin.* 'It's Henry, Miss!' she volunteered, pointing him out to the teacher.

But Miss Temple frowned. 'No, not that.

Something else; a kind of whirring sound.' She leaned across her bench towards the board duster, carelessly scrunched and pushed to one side.

Mandy saw Justin's grin expand. Vicki's face was ready to explode into laughter.

Miss Temple peered at the red checked duster. The faint whirring sound was definitely coming from under there. Gingerly she poked the duster, then raised a tiny corner. The whirring grew louder, like an angry bee.

Miss Temple gritted her teeth. She lifted the duster clear of the bench. A round, fat, hairy thing with eight long, spindly legs shot out from under it. Mandy stared wide-eyes. The 'thing' was a giant spider; a noisy, buzzing, creeping, squelchy, hairy-legged spider.

Vicki Simpson jumped to her feet for a better view. Becky held her back. Justin jumped on to his seat. The whole class was in uproar!

The spider shot across the bench, whirring angrily. It scrabbled across the length of the teacher's workbench and came up against a tall pile of textbooks, where it whirred and flailed.

'Hmm.' Miss Temple put on her best science teacher's voice. 'I suspect it's *Arachnis dunlophobia*, a very rare species indeed.' She poked at the spider with the sharp end of a pencil. It turned and sprinted back along the bench. A squeal shivered round the class.

Mandy squinted hard at the creature. Its grey, bumpy body was covered in ugly yellow blotches. It had big red eyes. Its legs, those long, hairy things, moved like clockwork. *Ah!* She caught Miss Temple's eye. *Clockwork*, she thought.

'Now, everyone, calm down and stand back. Justin, get down from that chair, please,' the biology teacher ordered. She went straight to the high shelf behind her desk and brought back a large, empty glass jar. 'I want to take this specimen alive.' Swiftly she trapped the spider inside the jar. A muffled whirring emerged. Legs scrambled helplessly against the glass. The spider tumbled and rolled. Then the whirring slowed and faded to a stop.

'Is it dead, Miss?' Justin demanded. He grinned at his twin sister.

Miss Temple winked at Mandy. 'No, Justin. *Arachnis dunlophobia* is a tougher species than that!' Carefully she lifted the jar and picked up the spider between thumb and forefinger. 'In fact, if we just wind this little knob here, I expect we'll soon revive him, no problem!' She smiled as she wound up the rubbery toy and placed him right way up on the bench once more. Sure enough, the spider began charging in straight lines up and down the bench.

'Oh!' Becky Severn sat back in her seat and fanned herself. 'It's a trick!' Vicki bit her lip, waiting to see how the teacher would react. Only Justin remained calm. Mandy saw him, standing hands in pockets, the grin fixed on his sturdy face.

Miss Temple raised her eyebrows at him. 'What a pity, Justin. I thought we were on to an exciting scientific discovery there. A Nobel prize at the very least.'

Justin kept on grinning. But when Miss Temple took the toy spider and placed it, legs still whirring away, inside her drawer, his smile began to fade. 'Hey, Miss, that's my spider!' he complained.

She cut him short. 'Yes, Justin, I know perfectly well it's *your* spider. But I think I'll just keep an eye on him for the rest of the day, if you don't mind. Now, you can make yourself nice and useful.' She picked up the duster and thrust it towards him in a cloud of chalk. 'Why don't you clean the board for me while I make my announcement? I'll have a word with you during break, *after* the bell has gone.'

Justin's mouth turned down, but Miss Temple had the upper hand. She hadn't panicked; she'd turned the joke against him. She waited until Justin settled into his task, then turned to the rest of the class.

Good for you, Mandy thought. Justin was well known as a loud-mouth and a bully. But Miss Temple had handled him well. She saw his twin sister sit back in her place, head down, unwilling to make eye contact. Gradually everyone settled down.

'It's about Henry,' Miss Temple began. 'We need to find him a good home for the school holiday.' A murmur ran round the room. The teacher raised both hands, asking for quiet. 'We need someone who can collect the cage after school tomorrow, take it home and look after him for six weeks. That means, preferably someone whose family is not going on holiday themselves, whom we can rely on to change the bedding every day, make sure that Henry gets his exercise and food, and a bit of regular company.' She paused while people considered this.

Mandy sighed and gazed at Henry. He'd stopped exercising and come out on to the floor of his cage to groom. His lovely marmalade-coloured coat shone in the sun. He stared back at her with his short sighted, twinkling dark eyes. His nose and whiskers twitched. *If only*, she thought. Looking after Henry for the summer would be fantastic. But it was out of the question. As vets at Animal Ark, her mum and dad had a rule that they would never take in extra animals; not strays, nor friends' cats and dogs, nor orphans from the wild. 'We're not a boarding-kennels, Mandy. We're vets,' her mum would say, kindly but firmly. 'No extra responsibilities, remember. We have enough as it is.'

Mandy reluctantly admitted that her mum and dad were right never to break their rule.

'This person must take great care to feed Henry his proper diet; cereal, rusks, nuts, fruit and vegetables, and not too many snacks!' Miss Temple paused to make the point about Henry's weight problem, then went on. 'There must always be clean drinking water in his cage. And you must be especially careful to keep it locked tight at night. Night-time is when pet hamsters get up to their tricks if you let them.

'So it's a responsible job, but if you feel you would like to have a go at looking after Henry, please write your name on a piece of paper as you go out of the lab. I'll take in all the names and put them into a hat. The one I draw out will be the lucky caretaker. I plan to make the draw early tomorrow morning, so please come and check to see if you've been lucky. If you are, you can take Henry home with you tomorrow afternoon.'

The end of the lesson bell went just as Miss Temple drew to a close. Chairs scraped on the floor, people picked up their bags and started to file out. Miss Temple took Justin into one corner for a stern word, then let him go. He shuffled out. Mandy sighed again as she noticed five or six people queuing up to give Miss Temple their slips of paper, Vicki Simpson and Becky Severn among them. She sidled by, towards the door.

'How about you, Mandy?' Miss Temple asked, knowing Mandy's love of animals. She brought her up short.

'Sorry, Miss. I can't.'

'Going on holiday?'

Mandy shook her head. 'No. It's just that we have enough animals to take care of as it is,' she said quietly.

'Ah.' Miss Temple nodded. 'So you can't manage it?'

Mandy shrugged, but an idea shot into her head as she glanced back at Henry, still preening in the sun. 'No,' she said, her spirits suddenly lifting. 'But I think I know someone who can!'

Two

'James!' Mandy cried. The corridor was crowded with kids, all making their way outside for morning break. She'd spotted her friend's serious face with its mop of straight brown hair and round glasses. 'Wait a second!' She squeezed through the crowd towards him.

He turned and gave her a shy grin. 'Hi, Mandy.' Then he whispered to a couple of friends to go ahead without him. 'Where's the fire?' he asked, as Mandy caught up with him at last.

'No fire. But listen to this!' she gasped. Her blue eyes were sparkling. 'You know Henry?'

'Henry who?'

'Henry the Eighth.'

'Yes, sure. He was the one with six wives, wasn't he? He kept killing them off for some reason.' James's eyes twinkling behind his glasses showed that he was teasing.

'No, not *that* Henry the Eighth. *Our* Henry, the school Henry! Henry the Hamster!'

'Oh, *that* Henry.' James folded his arms. 'I might have guessed it was an animal that you'd got so worked up about.'

Mandy felt people swarm by, knocking against her with their schoolbags, barging down the corridor, heading for the sunny playground. 'I'm not worked up!' she protested. Then she grinned at James. 'OK, then, I am. But listen, I've just had this terrific idea!'

James's brown eyes widened. 'Uh-oh!'

She grabbed hold of his elbow. 'Miss Temple needs someone to take care of Henry during the school holiday,' she gabbled. 'Well, of course I'd love to do it, but I can't, as you know, because Mum and Dad have this strict rule about pets, but I thought it would be terrific if *you* could take Henry home! Wouldn't it be great if you had him? I could pop in every now and then to help you look after him. Not that you couldn't manage perfectly well by yourself, I realise, but it would be *brilliant* if we both took care of him;

if you mum and dad say yes, and if you think it's a good idea too!'

'Whoa!' James put up both hands to fend Mandy off. 'Slow down.'

Mandy had only paused for breath. 'What's the matter? Don't you want to look after Henry? He's *gorgeous*! He's really, really friendly, and he's got a very interesting personality. Hamsters need company, and I'd be able to come nearly every day to help. It's not as if you'd have to do everything . . .' Mandy began to slow down. She felt herself go hot and red. Here she was, gushing on, and James was standing calmly in the emptying corridor, arms folded, a smile spreading across his face.

'Just hang on a minute,' he said slowly.

'Why? James, you have to make your mind up pretty quickly. Miss Temple is in the lab right this minute asking for volunteers. She's going to mix the names up in a hat and draw one out. She'll have finished and gone off to the staffroom if we don't hurry up!' Mandy's enthusiasm seemed to be falling on deaf ears. 'Don't you want to put your name on the list?'

James sprang his answer on her. 'I already have!'

'What?'

'We had biology first lesson. Miss Temple asked our class the same thing. I was the first to volunteer.'

'To look after Henry?'

James nodded, watching her puzzled face.

Mandy blushed even more furiously.

'Great minds think alike,' he told her. 'When Miss Temple said that Henry needed a home for the summer, I thought, me and Mandy, quick as a flash!'

They began to walk down the steps towards the playground. 'Do you think we'll be lucky?' she wondered. 'Henry seems to be pretty popular.' She glanced up and through the window at the queue of pupils still waiting to give their names to Miss Temple.

James shrugged. 'Think positive. There's always a chance that my name will be the one!'

'OK,' she smiled. 'So you'll go straight home tonight and ask your mum and dad if it would be all right?' The sun in the sheltered playground was almost hot enough to melt the tarmac. Mandy felt the heat, and fanned her face.

James nodded. 'Do you fancy a game of tennis after tea?'

'If it's not too hot,' she agreed.

They made their arrangements to go down to the courts by the riverside. 'Do you think they'll say yes?' she asked.

'About Henry?' He nodded. 'We already have Blackie and Eric to look after. What's one little extra hamster?'

Mandy smiled. Henry wasn't just any old hamster. She suspected he would be quite a handful. But Mr and Mrs Hunter weren't to know that. And anyway, there was no point counting your chickens before they were hatched; or your hamster before your name had been drawn out of the hat, she thought.

Mandy stretched out on the patio at the back of the cottage, letting her teatime food settle before she cycled down to James's house.

In the background she could hear the sharp barks and muffled yelps of some of the residents in the unit behind the surgery. This was where the patients stayed overnight at Animal Ark, recovering from operations, or perhaps for observation, until Mr or Mrs Hope had diagnosed their ailments.

Mandy yawned. The sun had sunk lower, but the evening was still warm. She could hear her father humming to himself as he fixed up the water hose and began to sprinkle the flower-beds in their long, rambling garden.

'*Summertime . . .*' he sang, low and soulful. '*And the livin' is easy . . .*' Adam Hope put on an accent that made him sound as if he came from the American South. Mandy lay back on her lounger and grinned.

> '*Boom-boom, b-boom . . .*
> *So, hush little baby,*
> *Do-on't you-u cry-y!*'

He sprayed water over limp patches of marigolds, oomp-pahing on an imaginary saxophone. Then with a grin he swung the hose round in Mandy's direction. Cold drops rained down on her white T-shirt and hot face. She squealed and leaped to her feet.

'Da-ad!' She put her hands over her head and darted off the patio on to the grass, seeking shelter behind the apple tree.

Adam Hope, holding the hose like a fireman in an emergency, squirted water at the tree.

'Mum, help!' Mandy squealed again. She saw Emily Hope appear at the French windows, stand-ing in her blue shorts and white sleeveless top, hands on hips, grinning at them. Mandy peered

out from behind her tree. The sunlight caught
in the spray, creating a million rainbow drops.
'Da-ad!' Mandy yelped again. She was soaked to
the skin.

Her dad pulled at the hose once too often.
It stretched and jerked, then came apart at a
point where a small metal clip held two sections
together. Water spurted out at Adam Hope,
gushing into the air and drenching him from head
to foot.

'Ha!' Mandy yelled, and staggered out on to the
lawn. Her sides ached from laughing. 'Serves you
right, Dad!' She watched water drip from his dark

hair and beard. 'That'll teach you to leave me to sunbathe in peace!'

On the patio, Mrs Hope quietly turned off the garden tap. She popped into the kitchen for two towels and came out and thrust them at her husband and Mandy. 'Never trust your dad with a hosepipe,' she warned, her face bright in the sun. 'He just can't resist pointing it at someone. Remember when you were little, Mandy? I'd get out the paddling-pool for you in the fine weather, and before I knew it, your dad would be out here in his swimming-trunks, offering to "fill it up" for me. I'd turn my back, and there he would be, squirting everyone in sight!'

Mandy laughed. Her dad sighed. 'You're only young once!' he pointed out.

'Exactly!' Mandy raised her eyebrows at her mum. She'd finished towelling her hair and spread the towel over a branch to dry.

'Which reminds me of a conversation I had with Sam Western in the surgery earlier this afternoon,' Mr Hope said, growing more serious. He put his arm round his wife's shoulder and the three of them wandered back towards the house. 'It was to do with enjoying yourself while you're young.'

Mandy only listened with half an ear. Sam Western owned a large farm up by High Cross. He lorded it over the district and made himself unpopular with his high-handed ways, but he was a man of influence in the village. Mandy didn't care for him, because he in turn didn't care much for the animals she loved. She gathered up her tennis things as her dad chatted on about Sam Western, ready to head off to James's house.

'. . . Apparently Sam Western intends getting up a petition. The town council has given permission for Bert Burnley to set up a caravan park for the summer in his bottom field. A school from Birmingham wants to run activity holidays for some of their kids. But Mr Western tells me there's a lot of local opposition . . . Mrs Ponsonby, Mrs Parker Smythe, the usual crew.' Mr Hope took off his wet T-shirt and wrung it out. Then he laid it to dry across the sun lounger.

Mandy gave her mum a quick kiss and told her where she was heading.

'What can they do about it if the council has already granted planning permission?' Emily Hope twisted her long red hair on to the top of her head and glanced up at the sun. She smiled and waved at Mandy. 'Don't be too late back,' she said.

'You know Sam Western. He won't take no for an answer. If *he* objects to this scheme for the caravan park by the river, then no mere town council can stand in his way. He's planning to have a sit-in or some such nonsense when the caravans arrive. And he asked me to sign his petition against the site being used as a temporary holiday centre. He says city kids will drag down the tone of the neighbourhood.'

Emily Hope frowned. 'You didn't sign?'

''Course not. I said he'd best be careful to stay on the right side of the law. If the council has said yes to the holiday centre, there's not much he can do about it.'

'What did he say?'

'He said they'd make the council pay more attention to what residents round here think.

There was a pause as Mandy unlocked the padlock on her bike and sat astride the saddle. The conversation had began to sound interesting at the mention of kids from the city coming to stay in Welford. A summer holiday centre? A caravan site by the river? This sounded like fun. There would be lots of new faces in the village; kids her own age.

'Well,' Mrs Hope said, her face set in determined lines. '*I'm* a local resident, and *I* think it's a great idea!'

'Me too,' Mr Hope agreed. 'Don't worry, I don't suppose even Sam Western can put a stop to it.'

'When will the caravans come on to the site?'

'The day after tomorrow; Saturday, I think.'

Mandy caught his last words, freewheeling down the drive towards the lane. She headed between high hawthorn hedges towards the village.

The Hunters' house stood close to the river, at the far end of Welford. As she cycled easily towards James's house, Mandy passed by a level field full of buttercups and daisies. At the far side of the field there was a fence and beyond that a slope down to the riverbank. It was a couple of acres, and occasionally the farmer, Bert Burnley, would turn a herd of Friesian cows on to it. But generally the field was left fallow, a haven for rabbits and moles; undisturbed, lush and overgrown. This was the field for the caravans, Mandy realised.

Even now there were two men clambering out of a small red pick-up truck, one with a sledgehammer, one with a white sign attached to a post. The words on the sign were clear for Mandy to read as she cycled by. 'RIVERSIDE CARAVAN PARK' it said in big black letters. The men angled the post into the ground by the edge of the field, and, as Mandy pedalled the final fifty metres to James's house, she heard the thud of the hammer as it drove the post into the hard ground.

Good! she thought. It was proof that the summer camp would go ahead. I wonder whether James knows he'll have a bunch of new kids staying opposite him? She rushed inside to tell him the news.

Three

'Great!' James agreed that the caravans were a good idea. 'I've always wanted to stay in one myself.' He grabbed his racket and they set off for the courts.

They arrived to find James's mum already there, playing a gentle game in the early evening against Mrs Parker Smythe from Beacon House. The Parker Smythes were rich neighbours of Sam Western, and Mandy wasn't surprised to hear the topic of conversation as the two ladies finished their game and came off-court to rest.

'I mean to say!' Mrs Parker Smythe's narrow voice rang out above the smack of tennis rackets against balls on nearby courts. She was cool and elegant in

her short white skirt, not a blonde hair out of place.
Mandy easily heard every word she said. 'Who knows
what sort of people we'll have coming to stay in the
village? And caravans are such a glaring eyesore.
Why, we might even be able to see them from our
house! And these children will all come from the
cities, and you can guess what they'll get up to
once they're let loose on a quiet little village like
Welford. Your house faces right on to the field,
doesn't it?' she asked James's mum. 'You must be
seething with anger!'

Mandy frowned as she trotted to the netting to
retrieve two balls. Mrs Parker Smythe was being her
usual snobbish self.

'Well, actually, no we're not,' Mrs Hunter said more
quietly. 'We weren't keen on the idea of caravans
when we first heard, it's true. But then we realised
it would be just for the summer, and we thought
what a lovely opportunity it was. Not just for the
children who will come here on holiday, but for
James and all the village children too. It's time they
broadened their horizons, don't you think?' She
looked Mrs Parker Smythe full in the face without
toning down her opinion. As she turned away to go
up the steps into the pavilion, she gave James and
Mandy a small wink.

'Well!' Mrs Parker Smythe stood there stranded. She swiped at the grass with her tennis racket and looked daggers at Mandy. 'There are plenty of people round here who take the opposite view!' she announced to nobody in particular, as she flounced up the steps after Mrs Hunter.

Mandy and James played fast and furious tennis, in spite of the heat. They called it a draw at one set each, promising to take up the challenge again next time. They flopped down by the netting to take a swig of orange juice which Mandy had brought along in her bag.

'How about an ice-cream?' James suggested.

Mandy nodded and they were soon on their bikes cycling back towards the village, past the newly erected sign.

'I'm glad your mum put Mrs Parker Smythe in her place,' Mandy said, glancing at the empty field. But she knew that Mr Western and Mrs Parker Smythe were not the sort to give in easily. She wasn't surprised to see a small knot of people gathered together up ahead, standing round the low silver car belonging to Mrs Parker Smythe which was parked just outside the post office in the centre of the village. She could hear arguments flying back and forth. Feelings were running high.

'I think it's an absolute disgrace!' Mrs Ponsonby proclaimed. Her Pekinese dog, Pandora, sat growling at her feet. 'The whole village will be swamped by strangers, and these city children aren't brought up to follow the country code! They'll leave gates open and sheep will wander on to the roads. They won't keep to public footpaths as they ought, and they will climb walls, you mark my words!' Somehow, the fusspot of Welford managed to make it sound like a hanging offence. 'And goodness knows what else they'll get up to!' she said darkly.

Mandy got off her bike and passed by the group, pausing to stroke Pandora and Mrs Ponsonby's lovable mongrel, Toby. Ernie Bell sat on the bench outside the post office, listening quietly. He shook his head. 'I reckon we should hold our horses before we all go overboard,' he warned. 'We musn't give a dog a bad name, you know.'

A strange, muddled picture of horses, ships and dogs jumbled in Mandy's mind, but she agreed with Ernie; the visitors should be given a fair chance.

She followed James into the cool, shaded interiors of the McFarlanes' shop to buy their ice-cream. When they came out, Mrs Parker Smythe was still gathering support for the anti-caravan campaign.

'Our first aim must be to stop them moving on to the site in the first place,' she ordered. 'It's all very well for Mr Burnley to wave his planning permission all over the place, but he's flying in the face of important local opinion.'

Mrs Ponsonby nodded. Toby, bored with the proceedings, trotted up to Mandy and sat with his tongue out, gazing longingly at her ice-cream.

'The first caravans are due to arrive on Saturday morning,' Mrs Parker Smythe went on. 'Our plan is to block their way in the lane. Mr Western will get his workers to drive tractors down and park across the gateway to the field. We must all be there to lend support!'

Ernie cleared his throat. 'And risk being carted off to the police station in Walton?' he said to the small crowd. 'It's against the law to obstruct a public highway, remember!'

Mandy and James agreed. She was concentrating so hard on the argument that her ice-cream cone tipped sideways, and the half-melted contents slipped out. But it had no chance to hit the ground; Toby caught it like a cricketer diving for a catch in the slips. He gobbled it in one gulp. Mandy's mouth dropped open in surprise.

'Shh!' James warned. If Mrs Ponsonby found out

she'd be rushing poor Toby straight over to Animal Ark with a near-fatal case of *frozen stomachitis*! Meanwhile, Pandora shuffled across to stare up at James's ice-cream.

'We must be prepared to stand by our principles!' Mrs Ponsonby took up the argument against the new caravans. 'We must make it clear that Welford is against changes of this sort, made without a by-your-leave.' She jutted out her double chin and pulled back her shoulders like a soldier on parade. The frills down the front of her powder-blue frock shook with outrage.

James slipped Pandora the remains of his ice-cream, cornet and all. He'd been won over by the Pekinese's huge, dark eyes. The ice-cream disappeared in a flash.

'Toby, Pandora, come here!' Mrs Ponsonby clapped her plump hands for their attention. 'Come here, good doggies!'

They both yawned and ignored her.

'Go on, Pandora. Go on, Toby!' Mandy whispered.

Reluctantly they obeyed her and trotted towards their owner.

Mrs Parker Smythe had started up the smooth engine of her silver car, and Mrs Ponsonby began to make her way up the street, head held high. People began to disperse, grumbling and muttering about the new caravan site.

Mandy looked at Ernie scratching his stubbly grey head. He gazed back at James and Mandy. 'Some folk round here don't have enough to do to keep them out of mischief,' he complained. 'And you know what they say; the devil makes work for idle hands.'

Soon the street was empty. As the sun began to sink, a golden red glow seeped into the sky. Mandy said goodbye to James, ready to head for home. 'Let's keep our fingers crossed,' she said, her mind flying back for a moment to the really important and interesting things in life: animals, and, more specifically, their hopes of looking after Henry.

'We'll find out tomorrow morning,' he reminded her.

'Let's go into school ten minutes early,' she suggested. 'To see if Miss Temple's picked out the name.'

They arranged to meet outside the post office at eight o'clock, then they rode off on their separate ways. James waved at Ernie and passed on by the new sign for the caravan site. Then he turned right, up his drive. Mandy rode up her lane towards the sunset, taking James's advice and thinking positive thoughts. 'We *will* be lucky,' she said over and over. 'We *will* be lucky and get to look after Henry for the summer!'

They gathered outside the biology lab before morning registration; Mandy and James, Vicki Simpson and her friend, Becky Severn, and Brandon Gill who lived at Greystones Farm. Altogether, Mandy counted twenty-three hopefuls, all waiting to see who would look after the school hamster.

She peered through the window into the empty lab. In one corner she spotted Henry's cage; a roomy, hardwood box with a removable glass front and a wire-mesh lid. Inside the box was a day area covered in fresh hay, with a drinking bowl in one corner. And there was a small 'upstairs' compartment; a box within a box, which Henry could enter via a sloping ramp. He used this private bedroom for his frequent daytime naps. And of course, in one corner was the exercise wheel.

Mandy could see him now, trundling away. He reminded her of a stout man jogging for his health, determined to get his daily exercise. She nudged James and pointed to the cage. 'Look at him,' she smiled.

'It will do him good,' he assured her. 'Did you

know, they found out that some hamsters run eight kilometres a night on those exercise wheels?'

Mandy let this sink in. 'Eight kilometres? Then why is he so fat?'

'I didn't say that *Henry* runs eight kilometres,' James pointed out. 'He probably just comes out to use the wheel when he knows someone's looking, to show off. I bet Henry just snacks and snoozes the night away!'

'Are you saying he's lazy?' Mandy pretended she wouldn't hear a word said against the hamster. 'If you ask me, it's not his fault he's so fat.'

'Whose is it, then?'

'It's all those people's who feed him crisps from their lunch boxes, obviously! You can't blame a poor little hamster for eating all the wrong, fattening foods, can you?'

'Hmm.' James looked thoughtful. 'I suppose not.'

Mandy nodded and looked up the corridor. 'Hurry up, Miss Temple!' she pleaded. She noticed Vicki Simpson whispering behind her hand to Becky. She ignored this and smiled at Brandon. 'How's Ruby?' she asked. Ruby was Brandon's pet pig.

'Grand,' Brandon said in his broad, no-nonsense way. 'We're going over to Walton this weekend to show her. We reckon we're in with a chance of a prize.'

Mandy was wishing him luck when Miss Temple appeared at the end of the corridor. She walked briskly towards them. Everyone fell silent. All eyes were on the young teacher as she unlocked the lab and invited them in.

'Sit down for a moment.' She put down her bag and turned towards them. 'Now, I haven't made the draw yet. I wanted you all to see that it's fair and above board.' She picked up a cardboard box. 'Since I haven't got a hat, this will have to do. All the names are in here on folded pieces of paper.'

Mandy fixed her eyes on the box. 'We *will* be

lucky!' she repeated silently to herself.

Miss Temple smiled at them all. 'We only have a few moments before the bell goes for registration,' she said. 'So who wants to pick the name out of the box?'

A forest of hands shot up.

'Becky, you're nearest. You come and do it for us.' Miss Temple held the box up above eye level so Becky couldn't see which paper she chose. 'Just reach up and draw one out. That's it.'

Becky stood on tiptoe. Mandy held her breath and kept her fingers crossed. She watched as Becky took a piece of paper from the box and handed it to Miss Temple. The teacher unfolded it and laid it flat on the bench. She looked along the rows. 'James Hunter,' she announced, clear as a bell.

James gasped. Mandy couldn't believe her ears. Several of the others smiled wistfully and shuffled off. Miss Temple held open the door and said sorry to the unlucky ones. But Becky frowned and muttered to Vicki, '. . . Seems a bit suspicious to me . . . can't be coincidence . . . Mandy is teacher's pet, we all know that . . . and James Hunter is her best friend!'

Vicki nodded. 'It was probably all a big fix.'

Miss Temple, busy now telling James where to find

her after school, overheard them. She turned to speak. 'Vicki, Becky, I'm sorry you're disappointed,' she said quietly. 'But so are about twenty other people. I can't let you go around school all day with those long faces. You just have to accept the luck of the draw.' She waited patiently until the two girls returned her gaze. 'That's better. And don't let me hear that you've been spreading false rumours that this was all done out of favouritism. It was nothing of the kind, as you very well know.'

Vicki and Becky blushed. 'Yes, Miss. Sorry, Miss,' they said.

'Well, go off to registration, and we'll hear no more about a fix. You too, Mandy and James, or else you'll all be in trouble for being late.'

They nodded and hurried down the corridor, hard on the heels of the two disgruntled girls. Only now could Mandy begin to believe their luck. She gave a little skip and a jump.

'What did I tell you about the power of positive thinking?' James grinned. They took the stairs two at a time.

'Pure luck!' Mandy teased.

'Says you!' Before he split off down a separate corridor, he paused. 'You know Henry's weight problem?' he reminded her.

She caught his eye. 'Can I guess what you're thinking?'

'I'm thinking fresh vegetables, dried oats, nuts and rusks!'

'No more crisps?' She began to smile. 'James, you're planning to put Henry on a diet!'

'A calorie count,' he confirmed.

'A strict regime.'

'An exercise plan, so we can bring him back in September looking like a new hamster. No more excess fat.' He grinned.

'Poor Henry.' Mandy shook her head. 'I suppose it's for his own good, though.'

'Poor Henry, nothing! My house is going to be the first hamster health farm in the country. What do you think, Mandy?'

She pondered the challenge. 'You're right,' she decided. 'No biscuits, no cakes!'

'Good. See you at four in the lab?' he asked. They would take Henry home together.

'You bet!' She sped off to her own classroom. They had Henry to themselves for the whole summer. They'd give him the best of everything, and make him stick to his healthy diet. They might even be able to take him on outings, down to the river for a picnic in the fresh air. Mandy made great plans. She sat at her desk just as her form teacher, Mr Meldrum, arrived. Her head was in the clouds, doting on Henry, when he called her name from the register.

'Mandy Hope?' he repeated sharply.

'Yes, Mr Meldrum!' she called. Four o'clock couldn't come soon enough. Then the whole summer holiday was spread before them; endless days of looking after Henry!

RIVERSIDE
CARAVAN PARK

Four

It was early Saturday morning. Mandy had been up
for ages, busy doing chores at Animal Ark before
Simon, their nurse, had even arrived. She cleaned
out cages and talked to the parrot, the gerbil and
the black Labrador who'd been kept overnight in
the unit. She knew that good hygiene was a top
priority for a vet, and anyway, she loved the company
of animals, talking to them and encouraging them
to get back on their feet after an illness.

Simon came in promptly at half-past eight to find
everywhere spotless and ready for surgery. He
chatted with Mandy for a few minutes while Jean
Knox, the receptionist, prepared the appointment

list. 'What's it feel like to have six whole weeks of freedom?' he asked.

'Brilliant!' Mandy bubbled with enthusiasm. She took off her white coat and hung it on a peg in one of the treatment rooms. 'James has brought home the school hamster for the holiday. We're going to take him down to the river for a picnic.'

'Lucky hamster,' Simon said with a grin. He was young and easy-going. 'I had a hamster when I was a kid. She was called Honey; a light golden one with beautiful ruby eyes. But she couldn't see a metre in front of her nose. Hamsters can't, you know. They're very short-sighted.'

Mandy nodded and made a mental note.

'They use their whiskers to feel their way about. They're nocturnal; dozy by day and active by night.'

Again Mandy nodded. 'Henry won't come to any harm if we take him on outings, will he?'

Simon smiled. 'He'll think he's in seventh heaven. I take it he's tame?'

'Very. He likes to be out of his cage. He sits in your hand and loves being stroked. And fed! That's his problem, actually.'

Simon smiled. 'Just watch what you give him to eat, that's all. No chocolate for a start. It's poisonous for hamsters. Apples are fine. Sunflower seeds are their favourite, and full of protein. They love biscuits and cake as well, but not too often.'

Mandy's face lit up. 'We plan to put him on a diet; fruit and greens, nuts and cereals. No sugar. We want him to lose weight.'

'Very good.' Simon followed her into reception and smiled at Jean, fixing his glasses firmly on his nose. 'Does Henry know about this slimming regime?'

'Not yet.' Mandy had reached the door, eager to be on her way down to James's house.

'Best of luck,' he called. 'And remember, be strict with Henry. Don't let him get round you with those big soft eyes. I know you!' He laughed as he watched her swing her leg over her bicycle saddle.

'Could you tell Mum I won't be back for lunch?' Mandy called before she sped off. 'Mrs Hunter's making us a packed lunch and we're taking Henry out for his treat!' She whizzed down the lane. The sun was still shining, the trees rustled in a slight breeze; a perfect day for a picnic.

Mandy lay flat on her back. The nearby river rippled and swirled, the sand was warm in the sun.

'Pass me another lettuce leaf for Henry,' James murmured. He sat cross-legged on the pebbles, with

the hamster nestled in the palm of his hand. Henry
was lazily grooming behind his ears with his tiny front
paws. His cage was set carefully to one side.

Mandy reached out an arm and felt for the hamper
which James's mum had packed. Her fingers made
contact with the wickerwork top. She flipped it open
and rummaged inside without raising her head to
look. Sun, sandwiches and lemonade had made
her sleepy.

James got up, balancing Henry in his hand.
'Don't worry, I'll do it. Anyway, why are you in such
a lazy mood?'

'I'll have you know I was up at the crack of dawn!'
she sighed. She opened one eye as James crouched
beside the hamper. Henry's nose and whiskers
twitched with interest.

'James, watch out!' Mandy sat bolt upright, but
her cry came too late. Henry had launched himself
from the palm of James's hand, straight into the
hamper. He landed with a thud amongst the leftover
biscuits. Real food! Beautiful calories! He tucked in
happily.

James panicked. He hadn't seen where Henry had
landed. 'Where is he? Quick, Mandy, where's he
gone?' He scrambled a few metres up the bank into
some long grass. 'Henry's escaped. Help me look!'

Mandy gazed down at a happy hamster. 'He's in here,' she said calmly. 'In the hamper.' She knelt for a closer look. 'Oh, Henry!' she scolded. She heard James creep up behind her. Together they peered into the shadowy safety of the picnic basket. Henry was nibbling biscuits to his heart's content. He munched and stored the crumbs in his cheeks, shoving biscuit into his mouth as fast as he could. Mandy glanced at James.

'Henry, the calories!' James stood his head.

'A fat lot he cares!' Mandy began to smile. 'And it's no good offering him lettuce now, not when there's a heap of broken biscuits to get at!'

Henry cocked his head at them. His bright eyes twinkled, his cheeks pouched out to twice their normal size.

'Come here, Henry.' James reached into the hamper and cupped both hands under Henry's fat little belly. He tried to sound severe, but a grin was spreading over his face too. 'So much for getting you slim! Oh, well, it could have been worse.'

'How come?'

'He could have actually made a run for it, I suppose. It would have taken us all afternoon to find him in that long grass. Thank heavens he landed in the hamper.'

Mandy shook her head. 'Henry knows which side his bread is buttered,' she said. Then she giggled.

'Or which way the cookie crumbles!' James laughed. 'But it's ruined his diet. We'll have to make him have an extra go on his wheel tonight, and nothing but lettuce for him tomorrow!'

Henry twitched his nose.

'I don't think he likes that idea.' Mandy watched James carry the hamster back to his cage. 'Time to be getting back,' she said. She tidied the hamper and closed its lid. 'I promised Dad I'd lend a hand with afternoon surgery.'

Henry's little escapade had brought them back to earth. It was all very well drifting through the sunny day on the riverbank like this, but there were jobs to do. She sighed as she stood up and straightened her T-shirt. 'Hey,' she said, glancing beyond the river into the field beyond. 'What's going on over there?'

There was a cluster of cars gathering on the narrow road. Two tractors came trundling down the lane after them, and a group of people stood by the gate into the field, talking loudly.

'It's that lot protesting about the caravans,' James said. He picked up the hamster cage and climbed on to the path. 'Mrs Ponsonby and the rest.'

Mandy spied a wide-brimmed pink hat in the

middle of the small crowd. And then she recognised
Mrs Parker Smythe's low, silver car. In the distance,
she saw a huge lorry with a trailer carrying the first
of the caravans. It crawled slowly towards the recently
formed roadblock. Voices rose. Someone brought
out a placard and raised it in the air.

'Come on!' Mandy said, picking up the hamper.
'Let's cut across and see what's going on!'

By the time they reached the gate, the protest was
well underway. A second lorry with its enormous load
had pulled up behind the first. James spotted
a police car bringing up the rear and pointed it
out to Mandy. 'Police escort,' he whispered. 'This
could be serious!'

But Mandy couldn't help smiling at the gang of
activists. They were an odd bunch to be breaking the
law. Mrs Parker Smythe, more at home at a cocktail
party, tried to look the part of a protester in a pair
of well-cut black trousers and a crisp white shirt. But
Mrs Ponsonby looked as if she was dressed for a
garden party in her flower-laden hat and
tight-fitting frock. Her stout face was red with the
effort of protest, as she waved her cardboard placard
high in the air. 'No Welcome to Caravanners in
Welford!' it said on one side, 'Welford Says No to
the Caravans!' on the other.

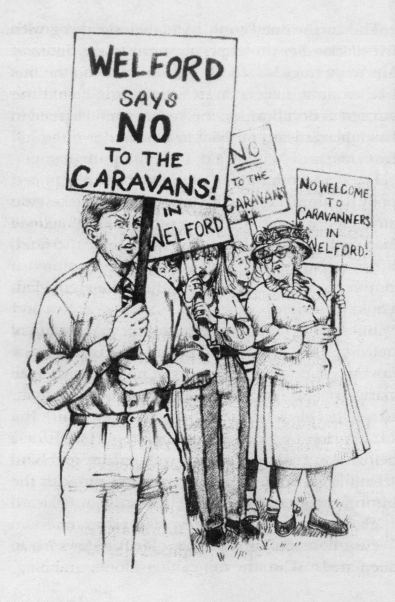

The two women took their orders, along with five or six other protesters, from the sturdy figure of Mr Western, who stood and directed operations like an army major. 'Watch your right flank!' he warned as Bert Burnley, the farmer who'd agreed to have the caravans on his land, came down the hill from his farm.

His Land-rover soon drew to a halt and he jumped out and strode across. He seized hold of the gate and let it off the latch. It swung free. Obligingly Mandy stood just inside the entrance to the field, holding it wide open.

'What's all the rumpus?' Mr Burnley growled. He was a thickset man with a wide, ruddy face and crinkly grey hair. 'Don't you know I've had council permission for this since Easter? Why not pack up and go home, or I'll get the police to act!' He glared at Sam Western, who strode towards him, hands on hips.

'Why don't you listen to what people have to say before you rush ahead with your money-grabbing scheme?' Mr Western shouted, centimetres from the burly farmer's angry face.

'Hear, hear!' Mrs Ponsonby chimed in.

'Now hang on just a minute.' Mr Burnley's frown deepened. 'Who are you calling money-grabbing,

Western? You'd best check your facts before you start accusing people!'

Mandy kept one eye on the arguing men, one eye on the approaching policeman. Behind the blue-uniformed figure she caught sight of a young, fair-haired reporter from the local paper, camera at the ready. She pointed him out to James. 'The newspaper's in on the act!' The row could develop into a local headline.

Mr Western snorted. His supporters rallied round, as the policeman, the reporter and two lorry drivers skirted around Western's tractors that were blocking the road.

'I said, check your facts,' Burnley roared. 'And you'll find I'm letting the caravans use this field rent-free. It's for a good cause, and I've told Kingsmill School to go ahead and give the kids a proper holiday, free of charge. It's time someone round here did something for nothing!' He squared up to Mr Western, red in the face. Mrs Ponsonby, Mrs Parker Smythe and the others looked taken aback.

'Hear, hear!' Mandy and James cried.

Mr Western blustered. 'Well, whether or not you're lining your own pockets, Bert Burnley, we still don't want the eyesore of a whole lot of caravans spoiling the look of the place. And we wont budge from here until you tell those lorry drivers to back off down that lane and take those trailers back where they came from!'

He didn't see the tall figure of the policeman loom up behind him, but Mandy and James did. They saw the reporter raise his camera and start to take shots of the protesters and their placards. They heard them fall quiet in the full glare of publicity. One or two crept away to their cars before they could be photographed.

'This will be in the paper on Monday,' someone whispered. 'I never bargained for that.' He went and sat quietly in his car, looking as if he wished the ground would swallow him.

But Mrs Ponsonby stood firm. She glared at the young policeman as he approached Sam Western and ordered him to tell his lads to move their tractors. 'Welford Says No!' she chanted.

The journalist wrote notes; Mr Western argued their case.

It was all to no avail. The policeman sternly pointed out that what they were doing was against the law. Mandy and James stood alongside Mr Burnley, happy to be photographed. 'We think it's a great idea,' Mandy told the reporter. 'Everyone should be able to come and enjoy the countryside.

We're looking forward to meeting these new kids. And I'd just like to say that not many people in Welford are against the idea of the caravan park. I think you should put that in your article!'

Mrs Parker Smythe overheard and tossed her head. Mrs Ponsonby glowered. But Mandy and James stood, one to either side of Mr Burnley, proudly facing the camera, under the bright new sign for Riverside Caravan Park.

'Thanks. It should make the front page on Monday,' the reporter told them.

'By the way, did you get Henry in the photograph?' Mandy asked. They watched as the policeman cleared off the protesters. Gradually the sit-in fell apart. Mrs Ponsonby stopped chanting and lowered her placard, Mr Western at last gave an order for the tractors to back off.

'Who's Henry?' The journalist packed away his notebook and camera, ready to dash off to file his report.

'The hamster.' Mandy pointed to the cage, where Henry stared contentedly at proceedings, his cheeks still pleasantly full of biscuit.

'Oh, yes; the hamster's in the shot, don't you worry,' the reporter said with a smile.

And so the protest faded. The protesters went

home, red-faced and grumbling, unused to losing an argument. Then the lorries trundled into the field with their huge caravans, while Mr Burnley shook hands with a young man and woman; two teachers from Kingsmill School who were organising the holiday centre.

'Thanks very much,' the young man said to Mandy, when he heard from the farmer the part Mandy and James had played.

Mandy blushed. 'We were glad to help.'

She and James said hello to the young woman, Chrissie Searle. The man was called Pete Cavendish. Both leaders were young and pleasant looking outdoor types in shorts and T-shirts. But they were too busy to stop and talk for long. 'The first batch of kids is due to arrive on Monday,' Pete Cavendish said. 'And there's loads to do before then.'

Satisfied, they went off their separate ways. Full of the latest news, James and Mandy went back to his house with Henry. Then Mandy hurried on home, passed the wooden sign with 'Animal Ark, Veterinary Surgeon' carved on it, and into the house to tell her mum and dad she'd be in the newspaper. The protest had collapsed, the caravans were moving in, and Mr Western had admitted defeat.

Emily Hope smiled and gave her a hug. 'That's

my girl!' she said after she'd listened to what
Mandy had said to the reporter. 'I couldn't have put
it better myself!'

Five

There was no doubt about it, Sam Western and his followers had made fools of themselves. Everyone at Animal Ark agreed that their picture on the front page of the newspaper on Monday morning made them out to be small-minded snobs. Mandy's own quote made the headline: 'A GREAT IDEA!' she read in bold, black capitals. Underneath the one of the protesters there was another good, clear picture of James holding Henry's cage, standing alongside Mr Burnley and Mandy, with a caption which read, 'Supporters of the caravan site.'

Mandy beamed across the breakfast table at her gran and grandad. They'd dropped in to show her the newspaper on their way back home from the village. Lilac Cottage, their pretty house, was down the lane from Animal Ark.

'So when do we expect the first arrivals?' Grandad asked.

'This morning. Pete and Chrissie have had to work like mad to get things ready. There are six caravans on the site, and a big Portakabin in the middle of the field, for a shop and clubhouse combined. They've got things really well organised now.'

'Pete and Chrissie?' Gran interrupted.

'Pete Cavendish and Chrissie Searle. They're the teachers from Kingsmill School in Birmingham.'

'And you're on first name terms already?' Gran teased.

'Yes. I think they're great. They plan to take the kids canoeing and mountain biking for a start, and if the weather stays fine, there's going to be a barbecue by the river at the end of the week!' Mandy was up on her feet, gulping down the last of her orange juice. 'Sorry, Gran, sorry, Grandad; I have to dash. I promised James I'd meet up with him in the village. We want to go and say hello to the first group when they arrive. Chrissie said she thought it would help to make them feel more at home. They're bound to find things pretty strange here in Welford if they come from a big city like Birmingham!'

She gave her grandparents a quick kiss and was on her way, grabbing her bike and whizzing down the lane.

James, ready and waiting in the yard outside the Fox and Goose, waved a greeting. 'I saw the Kingsmill mini-bus turn down our road five minutes ago,' he told her. They pedalled together down the main street.

Mandy nodded. 'How's Henry?'

'Great. He's back on his diet again; sunflower seeds and slices of apple. I left his cage in the fresh air on the front porch. Mum says she'll keep an eye on him.'

They cycled easily and quickly along the flat stretch of road. Up ahead, over the tops of the hawthorn hedges, they could see the gleaming new caravans in Mr Burnley's field.

'OK?' Mandy asked. They propped their bikes against the gatepost and went into the field.

She felt suddenly shy as she stepped through the long grass towards the grey Portakabin. But she thought how much more strange things must seem to the newcomers who sat on the grass outside the hut, looking warily at her and James as they approached.

'Hi,' she said to a sea of faces; a dozen or so kids of about her own age, some propped back on their elbows, some lounging against the wall of the hut, some pretending not to notice her and James. Mandy saw one girl standing apart from the rest. She was small and skinny, with wild red hair and grey-green eyes. 'I'm Mandy Hope,' she said. 'I live here in Welford.'

The girl stared shyly back. She nodded, but didn't open her mouth to speak.

'Never mind her,' one boy said. 'You can't get a word out of her. Anyone fancy a game of footie?' He picked up a white plastic ball and rolled it into the space in front of the hut.

Several voices chorused 'Yes.' James nodded, glad to join in. Soon the ball was being booted up and down the field to the sound of excited yells, calls of foul and claims for penalty kicks.

Mandy grinned at the shy girl. 'Who's the boy with the football?' she asked. He dribbled the ball expertly and passed it, shouting out instructions.

'Paul.' The answer came out almost a whisper.

'And who's the girl with the blonde hair?'

'Sonia.'

Mandy tried her best to commit their names to memory. 'Who are you?'

'Leanne Jackson.' The girl delivered her own name with a blush that coloured the whole of her face. 'I'm new at Kingsmill.'

'Are you all from the same school?'

'Yes, but I've only been there since May. My mum and me had to move house. That's why I changed schools again.'

Mandy went carefully ahead. She glanced at Leanne, then back at the football game. 'My mum's got the same colour hair as you. Only, she's not my actual mum. My real mum and dad died in an accident just after I was born. I'm adopted.'

Leanne raised her eyes from the buttercups at her feet and stared at Mandy. 'Have you got a dad?'

Mandy nodded. 'He's the local vet. So's my mum. He's lived in Welford all his life.'

A sigh escaped from Leanne. 'A vet? Have you got loads and loads of animals at your house?'

'Sort of. Only, they're not mine; they're patients at the surgery. Dogs, cats, rabbits, donkeys, ponies; you name it. Oh, and I do have three pet rabbits of my own.'

Leanne sighed again. 'Lucky thing.'

'Don't you have any pets?' Mandy was happy to chat on about her favourite subject. The two of them sat down cross-legged on the grass, one eye on the

noisy game. Sonia, in goal, saved one of Paul's shots.
A fresh cheer went up.

'No, I'm not allowed,' Leanne said. 'My mum and
me live in a flat, and we can't keep pets.'

Mandy said she thought it was a shame. Behind
her shyness, Leanne seemed friendly and easy to talk
to.

'I'd love to have one,' she went on wistfully. 'A pet
all of my own to look after, I mean. I've always wanted
to. But we move around too much. My mum says it
wouldn't be fair on any animal.'

'I suppose so.' Mandy thought for a second. 'Listen,
Leanne, why don't we go over to James's house? I'm
sure he won't mind, and there's something I'd like
to show you. He lives just across the road; it won't
take long!'

Slowly, awkwardly, Leanne got to her feet. 'OK.'

'Great!' Mandy led the way out of the field, across
the narrow road. They jogged past Claire MacKay's
house, where the sign for 'Rosa's Refuge' hung from
a tree in the garden. 'Claire looks after hedgehogs,'
Mandy explained. 'She's quite new to the village, but
she soon settled in once she'd set up the refuge.'
She smiled at Leanne as they went through James's
gate and up the garden path.

James's Labrador must have heard their footsteps,

for he came bounding down the side of the house, tail wagging. Mandy gave him a hug. 'This is Blackie,' she said to Leanne. 'And the little cat asleep on the mat is Eric.'

Leanne went up the step and bent to stroke his soft, warm head. Eric purred. 'He's lovely,' she sighed.

Mandy pointed to the wooden cage on a shelf in the front porch. 'And this is Henry.'

'A hamster!' Leanne's eyes lit up. 'Oh, he's gorgeous!'

Henry, aware of his admiring audience, responded by jumping into the exercise wheel. He set it in motion with his feet, easily keeping his balance as he trundled away.

'He's a golden hamster. He's six months old. He belongs to our school, but James is looking after him for the holiday,' Mandy explained, glad to see Leanne's face beaming down at Henry. 'Do you know much about hamsters? They're desert rodents. They're hoarders.' She reeled off the facts.

'I know. Born in a litter of six to ten infants, without hair. Eyes open on the twelfth day. Life span two to three years.'

'Hey!' Mandy was impressed.

'I've read all about them in my pets book. But I've never actually been this close to one before.' She gazed into the cage as Henry clambered out of the wheel and came up to the front of the cage, whiskers twitching.

'Would you like to hold him?'

Leanne nodded. She held her breath as Mandy cupped her hands under Henry, lifted him out of the cage and gave him to her. Henry nibbled her finger, then nestled contentedly in her palm. 'Oh!' she said, speechless.

'I expect you'll be able to come and see Henry whenever you like,' Mandy promised. 'James won't mind. And I come down here most days, to help look after him. Staying at Riverside means you're really close at hand.'

With her free hand Leanne stroked Henry's golden coat. 'He's so soft! His feet tickle!'

'Try giving him this.' Mandy handed her a slice of apple from a plastic bag on the shelf. She watched as the hamster took it and began to nibble. They both smiled.

At last, Leanne reached forward to put Henry back in his cage. 'I'd better be going.' The smile had begun to fade.

'But you'll come again?'

'Yes, please.'

Mandy fastened the lock. Leanne took a last look at Henry, then stroked Eric as Mandy went to play in the garden with Blackie. Just then, Mrs Hunter stuck her head through the kitchen window and waved. 'Hello, Mandy!'

'Hi, Mrs Hunter. This is Leanne Jackson from Birmingham.'

'Hello, Leanne. Nice to meet you. I hope you have a good time here in Welford.' Mrs Hunter smiled and turned back to Mandy. 'Can you tell James to come home for lunch at twelve-thirty?'

Mandy promised: then she and her new friend headed back for the caravan field. By the time they got there, the football game was coming to an end, with a three-two victory for Paul's team. Leanne nodded quietly at Mandy and slipped away to her caravan before the crowd of thirsty players charged up to the shop for cans of Coke.

James, already part of the gang, introduced Mandy to Ben, a tall boy with bristly hair. Ben was a joker, and obviously fashion-mad. He wore all the latest sports gear, pleased to have the others looking up to him. Mandy smiled and settled in with the crowd, soon forgetting about lonely Leanne.

'What shall we do now?' Sonia demanded with a yawn. She came out of the shop and flopped to the ground. 'Not much going on round here, is there?'

Her friend, Marcie, sprinkled a handful of daisy

petals in her hair. 'Stop moaning, Sonia.' Marcie's broad face was cheerful and friendly. She grinned up at Mandy. 'She never stops complaining, that's her problem.'

'Yes I do. The country's boring, that's all!' Sonia stared at the hillside. 'Nothing happens. No shops, no coffee bars. I don't know why I said I'd come!'

'See!' Marcie laughed.

'Aagh, what was that?' Sonia squirmed and tried to wriggle one arm up the back of her T-shirt. 'Something's alive in there! Ouch! Get it out, Marcie!' She sprang up, yelping and dancing around in panic.

'Stand still then!' Marcie giggled. She fished about and pulled a flattened daisy from under her friend's shirt. 'Very alive, I'm sure!'

Sonia scowled and flounced off to her caravan. 'Well! Anyway, I hate the countryside!' she wailed.

Mandy turned to Ben, who was trying to persuade a red-eyed boy called Sean to go swimming in the river. 'James says it's not that deep. And I bet it's dead warm! Come on, what are we waiting for?'

'I dunno.' Sean frowned. 'I think I'm allergic to something round here.' His light brown hair flopped over his forehead, his brown eyes streamed.

'Hay fever?' Mandy suggested.

Sean groaned. 'Call this a holiday? Just stick me

down on a beach somewhere hot like Spain or Greece, will you? I can't stand all these flowers!'

'There's a beach by the river,' James suggested. 'And if you stay by the water, your hay fever won't be so bad.' He ran ahead, followed by Ben and a reluctant Sean.

Mandy watched the field empty, as all the Kingsmill kids went off in different directions. They were a mixed bunch, and they hadn't all settled in yet, but she'd taken to Leanne from the start. She hoped to see her again soon. Waving at Chrissie Searle inside the shop, Mandy went to get her bike and rode slowly back to Animal Ark.

By early Wednesday morning, Mandy found that the freedom to come and go as she pleased had really sunk in. She loved the feeling of not being tied to school routine. It meant she was able to help out more at the surgery, and to ride her bike around the village, or to visit friends up on farms.

But there was already gossip in the village about the children at Riverside. There was tittle-tattle in McFarlane's when Mandy popped in for postage stamps for her gran. Mrs Ponsonby was in the thick of it, of course, advising Susan Price not to get mixed up with the newcomers. 'They're a thoroughly bad lot,' she warned. 'I'm sure your parents wouldn't want you to mix with them, Susan dear.'

Susan was in her riding gear. She made a secret grimace at Mandy. 'Thanks, Mrs Ponsonby,' she said breezily. 'Anyway, I'm riding Prince in the gymkhana over at Kenley next week, so I've got a lot of work on my hands to get him up to scratch.'

'Quite right; keep you out of mischief.' As the shop bell rang and Susan made her escape down the steps, Mrs Ponsonby turned to Mr McFarlane to report the latest wrongdoings of the city children. 'They've been here less than three days, and already they've caused havoc in the village! They have left gates open, of course, and it had to be on poor Mr Western's land, just as I said, and Dennis Saville had to round up several cows from the moor road. It's a wonder none of the poor beasts was injured!'

'Are they sure it was the children from Riverside, Mrs Ponsonby?' Mr McFarlane slowly weighed out a hundred grammes of mint toffees.

'Of course. Mr Western saw them with his own eyes. And the noise from the site is dreadful. Loud music until late at night. Wild games. Shrieking and shouting and playing in the river. I shouldn't be surprised if someone were to drown!' Mrs Ponsonby took off her pink-framed glasses and wiped them on a tiny lace handkerchief. She fixed them primly back on her nose, then turned to Mandy. 'You can't say I didn't warn you!' she said in triumph.

Mandy bit her tongue. 'Five first class stamps please,' she said to the shopkeeper, as Mrs Ponsonby took her bag of sweets and sailed out of the shop.

She must have been scowling because Mr McFarlane winked and said, 'Take no notice.'

'That's all very well, but other people might believe what she says,' Mandy grumbled. She didn't want Mrs Ponsonby to spoil things for the Riverside crowd. So far, they had enjoyed their mountain biking and canoeing activities, and there had been no major incident, but Mrs Ponsonby and Mrs Parker Smythe kept their eagle eyes constantly open, and Mr Western was poised to send off his petition to the council at the first sign of real trouble. Mandy paid her money for the stamps and made her way out with a shake of her head.

But she was stopped in her tracks by a scene in the heart of the village. A group, including Ernie Bell and his friend, Walter Pickard, with Betty Hilder from the animal sanctuary and Mandy's friend John Hardy from the pub, had gathered by Walter's garden wall. In their midst, Mrs Ponsonby stood examining fresh evidence.

'You say they were standing on your wall-top?' she asked in a loud voice.

They stared at something lying at their feet. With a sinking heart, Mandy got off her bike and went to take a look.

'Same as always,' Walter agreed. 'It's a nice sunny position, see.'

Peering over the wall, in amongst the feet of the bystanders, Mandy could see the remains of clay flowerpots, scattered earth, and half a dozen uprooted geranium plants. They were all trampled into the flagstones in Walter's yard. She glanced up at the old man's dismayed face. She knew he tended his plants with care. The geraniums brightened up the row of little stone cottages year after year, and Walter could hardly afford to replace them at this time. Whoever had done this must have been acting out of mischief, not knowing how much the flowers meant to him.

'Did you see who did it?' Ernie asked, his voice tense with annoyance.

Walter shook his head. 'I just opened the door to collect my milk from the step and there they were, all smashed!'

'It's obvious,' Mrs Ponsonby told them. 'Didn't I tell you that those children from the caravan site were running wild? I knew there's be some serious damage before too long!' She fixed them with her beady eyes.

'But you can't be sure,' Betty Hilder objected. 'Not if Walter didn't actually see them do it.'

'It stands to reason. We never had a moment's trouble in the village before those young hooligans came along. Now every day there's something new. Cattle on the loose. Loud late-night parties. And now vandalism!' Mrs Ponsonby let this last word roll richly round her tongue.

'Hmm.' Walter shook his head. 'Whoever it is, it won't stick them pots back together, and it won't revive them poor geraniums neither.'

'But I did try to warn you all,' Mrs Ponsonby insisted. 'I knew that the caravan site spelt trouble, only none of you would listen.' She sniffed and glared at Mandy. 'Well, I hope you're satisfied!' she said, stalking off down the street.

Shaken, Mandy couldn't find the nerve to defend the city children in front of poor Walter. Betty ran to the pub for a broom to begin clearing up the mess, while Ernie took his friend to his own cottage for a cup of tea.

It's only a few flowers, Mandy told herself, and nobody even knew for sure whether they'd been upset by accident or on purpose. But she knew it looked bad. The campaign to get the caravans turfed out would latch on to just this kind of mystery.

'Do you really think it was them?' John Hardy whispered to Mandy. His studious face waited earnestly for an answer.

'No, I don't,' she said slowly. 'But try telling that to Mrs Ponsonby!'

She sighed and rode off. There was trouble brewing, and, if the anti-caravan campaigners got their way, the Riverside children would be made to feel even less welcome than before!

Six

By Thursday afternoon, Mrs Ponsonby, Mr Western and Mrs Parker Smythe had succeeded in rousing half the village into a state of outrage over a few broken flowerpots.

'Poor Walter Pickard!' Mrs Ponsonby wailed, buying her daily ration of mint toffees from McFarlane's. 'He cherished those geraniums!' Mandy caught the gist of her remarks through the open door of the post office. She was posting letters for her gran, before she headed home to help in the surgery.

'It should never have been allowed in the first place!' she heard Mrs Parker Smythe tell Reverend

Hadcroft. Mandy arrived home and propped her bike against the surgery wall, then went into reception. Mrs Parker Smythe and her daughter, Imogen, were coming out, as Reverend Hadcroft went in with his cat, Jemima.

'I don't mean to be uncharitable, vicar, far from it, but I *knew* the caravan site would mean trouble for the village. Why, only this morning I saw a whole horde of those children career past our house on those mountain bike things. And the two leaders are almost as bad as the children. They couldn't keep control of a kindergarten, never mind a bunch of unruly teenagers!' Mrs Parker Smythe was hard to ignore, in her brilliant turquoise dress and gold jewellery.

Mandy saw Imogen sigh and hold tighter to the cardboard box containing her twin rabbits, Button and Barney.

Reverend Hadcroft smiled back. 'I'm not sure that *control* is what it's all about, Mrs Parker Smythe. After all, the children have come to Welford on holiday. They're bound to let their hair down.'

'Oh, so you call destroying an old man's prize geraniums letting their hair down?' Mrs Parker Smythe retorted. She turned and seized the attention of Mrs Platt, who happened to be walking up to the surgery with her miniature poodle, Antonia. 'Did you hear the news, Mrs Platt? The caravan children were let loose on their bicycles up on the moor near High Cross. No thought of sticking to public rights of way, mind you. Oh no, Sam Western had to threaten them with his dogs unless they kept off his land!'

Mrs Platt looked worried. 'Things seem to be getting out of hand. I must warn Vicki and Justin. They're staying with me for a few days, while their mum and dad are away and I want to keep them out of trouble. You can't be too careful with young people these days.'

Mandy realised that Mrs Platt was the Simpson twins' great-aunt. She lived in a bungalow in a small modern estate and occasionally had Justin and Vicki to stay.

She watched Reverend Hadcroft ease his way past, and stopped for a moment longer to listen as the two women gossiped on.

'I felt so sorry for old Walter,' Mrs Platt went on. 'I saw him sitting on his bench outside the pub last night, poor chap, and he didn't look at all like his usual cheerful self.'

Mandy had heard enough. She gave Imogen a smile, and went inside. Her mind was still on the thorny problem of the Riverside children as she put on her white coat and went to help her dad with the vicar's cat.

'Ah, Mandy, I've already sedated Jemima, and now we just need to take a quick X-ray,' Mr Hope said. 'Lift her into position so we can take a picture of her tail; that's right. It looks as if she's done it some serious damage, I'm afraid.'

The vicar looked on anxiously as they carried out the X-ray on poor Jemima. 'I noticed her tail was drooping as soon as she came in this lunch-time. She wasn't her usual self at all, so I brought her straight here.'

'Quite right.' Adam Hope took the plate out of the machine a few minutes later. 'Look, Mandy, can you see a hairline crack across the vertebra here? About six centimetres from the tip? It's a fracture.'

Mandy looked hard at the X-ray, then nodded.

'It looks like Jemima may just have used up one of her nine lives,' Mr Hope told the vicar. 'She's had a narrow escape, by the look of things.'

'What will you do?' He stroked his cat and whispered gently to her, as she began to raise her head and take notice. The sedative was wearing off.

'We'll have to perform a minor operation to remove the tip of the tail. The fracture has paralysed the nerve supply. But don't worry, cats manage perfectly well without their tails. In fact, she probably won't even notice after a day or two.' Mr Hope picked her up and gave her to Mandy. 'We'll keep her in overnight and do the job in the morning, OK?' He told Mandy to take the cat into the residential unit and make sure she was put safely inside one of the cages.

Mandy gave Jemima five-star treatment. She put an extra padding of newspaper around the base of a clean cage, to stop her from banging the useless tip of her tail. She made sure she was warm and settled. By the time Mandy got back to the treatment room, Mr Hope had seen his last patient, and surgery was finished.

Now she had time to consider what to do about the Riverside problem. She told her dad about it. 'Do you think they're going round deliberately upsetting people?'

'Do *you*?'

Mandy shook her head. 'I think forgetting to shut Mr Western's gate must have been a mistake, pure and simple.'

'And what about Walter's flowerpots?'

She paused. 'I think the Riverside crowd are innocent until proved guilty,' she decided. 'I can't see that there's any concrete evidence against them!'

Her dad smiled. 'Have you thought about becoming a lawyer when you grow up?'

Mandy laughed. 'Oh no, thanks. Give me animals any day!' She wanted to be a vet, like her parents.' I think I'll just pop down to James's to see what he thinks.' She took off her white coat. 'And to see Henry, of course!'

'Of course. How's his diet plan going?'

'Pretty good. His weight's down to a hundred and thirty grammes. James weighs him every morning on the kitchen scales!'

'Excellent. Keep up the good work!'

She went off with a smile and a wave, thinking hard about how they could help Sonia, Marcie, Ben, Paul and the rest.

'What's up?' James asked. He'd been building Henry a playpen on the lawn out of four long planks and four bricks. The planks formed a square, propped in position and held upright by the bricks. It gave Henry a large, safe exercise area. He frolicked inside it as Mandy came into the garden.

'Mrs Ponsonby and Mrs Parker Smythe; that's what's up!' She flung herself on to the grass. 'They're dead set on blaming the Riverside kids for every single thing that goes wrong around here!' She told him the latest mishap with Walter's geraniums. 'I wish Mrs Ponsonby wouldn't jump to conclusions,' she complained. 'And I wish Mr Western wouldn't set his guard dogs on trespassers. People might not know they're on private property.'

James nodded. 'Have you seen anyone at Riverside today?'

'Not yet. I think most of them went mountain biking again. Has Leanne called?'

'I don't think so. I want to show her Henry's new play area. What do you think?'

'Brilliant!' Mandy began to smile. 'And by the look of it, Henry thinks so too!' The hamster was scampering from corner to corner, then sitting on his haunches and combing his whiskers. 'And I think he's actually *looking* thinner, James! You're getting him into really good shape!'

James smiled proudly. 'The extra exercise will help too.' He took a plastic dish full of clean water and placed it inside the playpen. Henry twitched his nose, bent his head, and trotted to the dish. 'Just keep an eye on Henry, will you, Mandy? I want to go inside and get a bit of hard-boiled egg. He loves it.'

Mandy lay full length on the warm grass, propping her chin in her hands, as James went off for Henry's healthy snack. His garden was lovely and peaceful. She could hear the bees buzzing from flower to flower, birds singing in the trees overhead. Lazily she gazed at the hamster as he explored the lawn for grubs and insects.

She looked up when she heard a faint new sound coming from behind the high hedge. Voices yelled, short and sharp. Someone or something came running along the lane in the afternoon heat. The footsteps grew nearer. Mandy peered through the hedge and caught a glimpse of a striped blue and white T-shirt. She raised herself to her knees to see who it could be.

The figure stopped running just outside James's garden. Mandy heard someone quietly sobbing, and then she saw a girl's face looking back at her through the green hedge. When she saw she was being watched the girl backed off and disappeared.

Footsteps started up again, heading across the road, then rustling through long grass towards a small wood opposite James's house. But Mandy had seen a flash of flaming red hair, and she guessed that the pale face and sob's belonged to Leanne. She sprang to her feet to follow her.

Out in the lane, as she checked the road for cars, Mandy spied two more figures heading towards her.

She recognised Justin and Vicki Simpson, the twins from school. They were walking Antonia, their aunt's poodle, but when they saw Mandy they hesitated.

Mandy frowned. From the grins on the faces of the pair, she guessed they were the ones who'd upset Leanne and sent her crying into the woods. By now, her blue and white T-shirt had vanished between the slender trunks of the larch trees, so Mandy turned to wait.

'Hi, Mandy.' Justin chewed the juicy end of a grass stalk and slouched along, hands in pockets. Vicki was letting the poodle strain at the leash. The little dog was panting and pulling in the heat. 'We fancied looking in on old Henry.'

'Feel free.' She cast a worried glance after Leanne. 'He's on the lawn.' She met Vicki's unblinking gaze. 'James has just gone inside to fetch him a snack. Don't let Henry out of his playpen, will you?'

Vicki tossed her head. Her bobbed brown hair swung back. Her solid, sunburnt arm reached out and pushed open the gate to James's garden. 'As if!' she retorted. Then she carelessly let go of Antonia's lead and the dog scampered across the grass towards the hamster's playpen. She had her nose to the ground and dragged the red leather lead behind.

'Watch out!' Mandy shouted a warning to James,

who had just come out on to the porch with Henry's snack. James looked up, then leaped down the steps to head Antonia off. The poodle yapped. Blackie, shut up in the kitchen while Henry was out to play, set up a frenzied racket. Eric, snoozing on the mat, stood up, arched his back and hissed.

James zipped across the lawn like lightning. He scooped Henry out of danger, just as Antonia bounded into the middle of the playpen. Vicki charged after her, knocking planks flying as she seized the runaway's lead. Meanwhile, Mandy fumed at Justin, who stood propped against the gatepost, doubled up with laughter.

'It's not funny!' Mandy protested. 'And neither is upsetting Leanne Jackson. What did you say to her?' If she'd stopped to think things through, she probably wouldn't have challenged Justin, who liked putting people down whenever he had the chance.

'Oo-oh!' he replied. 'No need to get upset!' He stood free of the gatepost. 'We're touchy all of a sudden, aren't we?'

Mandy swallowed hard. 'No, I'm not. I just think we should give the Riverside kids a chance to enjoy themselves. Everyone gets on at them as if they were criminals or something!' Her eyes blazed. By now Antonia's yapping had died down and Vicki had firm hold of the lead. She wanted to stroke the hamster, so James held him out for inspection. Henry seemed none the worse for his close shave.

'Well, according to my aunt, that's just what they are, a load of vandals,' Justin sneered. 'It's all she's been on about since we first got here. They wrecked a whole lot of old plant-pots, didn't they? And she says she bets the kids that come next week won't be any better, or the ones the week after that.' He seemed to enjoy the idea of other people getting into trouble. His lazy, lip-curling grin spread from ear to ear as he sauntered across the lawn towards his sister.

Mandy was still furious. She couldn't trust herself to stick around any longer. So she cut off across the lane towards the woods, knowing that now there was little chance of tracking down Leanne.

Sure enough, the sun filtered through the spiky, bright green leaves of the larch trees, the sweet smelling ground was soft and silent in the shadows, but Leanne had disappeared.

Seven

'Let's take Henry for a little walk,' James suggested that evening.

Mandy had been staring into space. She sat on James's garden swing with the hamster asleep on her lap, but she jumped at the idea. 'Down to Riverside,' she suggested. Henry woke up and shook his whiskers. He blinked sleepily in the evening sunlight. 'We could see if we can find Leanne and let her have a chat with Henry.'

The memory of the red-haired girl slipping away into the wood, her face pale and tear-stained, refused to fade from Mandy's mind. After the first, friendly visit, when Leanne had left the others playing football and come with Mandy to meet the hamster, they hadn't seen as much of her as they'd hoped. The shy girl had popped in once or twice with healthy treats for Henry, but the village gossip seemed to have affected her badly. She seemed to want to hide whenever Mandy saw her; in the village or strolling by the river. She still looked lonely and unhappy, and now this episode with the Simpson twins had probably made things worse. 'I wonder what they said to her,' she muttered, lifting Henry and easing him into his cage.

James locked it securely. 'Who?'

'The twins. To Leanne. I'm sure they upset her.' She told him about the running footsteps and the sobbing.

'Trust them!' James lifted Henry's cage and together they set off for the caravan site. 'Is that what's been on your mind?'

Mandy nodded. 'I suppose so.' They crossed the road and cut diagonally across the field towards Riverside. 'It's bad enough Leanne feeling she doesn't fit in with the Kingsmill crowd, without coming here on holiday and being treated like this!'

James agreed. 'Let's hope Henry will be able to cheer her up a bit.' They climbed a stile over a dry-stone wall into the field where the gleaming white caravans stood.

Chrissie Searle was the first to wave a friendly greeting. 'Hi, I'm just off over to Walton for barbecue bricks,' she told them. 'We're having a party tomorrow night. Would you like to come?' She stood, one foot on the mini-bus step, ready to haul herself up on to the driving seat. In the space of a week, the sun had lightened her short, blonde hair and tanned her long limbs. She gave them a quick grin. 'If you're still willing to associate with the likes of us, that is!'

Mandy grinned back. 'Just try and stop us!'

'Good. Seven-thirty tomorrow evening, then!' Chrissie climbed up and started the engine. 'See you there.'

The mini-bus drove off and Pete Searle came out of the camp shop. He strolled across, followed by a few of the children. Soon Mandy, James and Henry were part of the crowd. Marcie handed round her bag of crisps. Paul produced his football and began a game, while Sonia settled down and told Mandy a tale of being woken in the middle of the night.

'It was pitch black, honest!'

Mandy sat on the grass with Henry safe inside his cage, ready to listen.

'The dead of night. I wake up, and there's this *bump-bump-bump* noise right outside the caravan!' Sonia's grey eyes widened as she told her story, and her voice dropped to a whisper. 'I was scared to death, I can tell you! I dig Marcie in the ribs to wake her up. Leanne's already sitting up in bed wide awake.

'This thing, whatever it is, is going *bump-bump-bump* and the whole caravan starts to rock. I stuff the pillow in my mouth to stop myself from screaming. Even Marcie closes her eyes and clings on to me.

'But Leanne just gets out of bed, goes across and flings open the door like it's broad daylight out there! There are these huge, white, rolling eyes staring in at us. I think I'm going to faint. But Leanne starts saying, "There, there," and making these clicking noises with her tongue. By this time I've got my hands over my eyes and I can hardly breathe, I'm so scared. But when I take a peep, there's Leanne going for sugar lumps in the bowl and handing them to this ginormous thing that's snorting and breathing all over us. He's halfway up the steps by now!'

Mandy burst out laughing. 'What was it, then?'

'A giant horse! Grey. Well, sort of ghostly white in the moonlight. Apparently it had got in from the next field. But Leanne didn't turn a hair. She stroked its neck and talked nicely to it. Then she went off to take it safely back to its field. And the thing is, when she came back she was actually looking happy, like she'd enjoyed the whole thing!'

'Where is she now?' Mandy looked round, beyond the noisy game of football, towards the river.

'Who, Leanne? Don't ask me. She's probably wandered off somewhere by herself again. It's a pity, really. Me and Marcie, we think she's OK, only she's hard to get to know, she really is.' Sonia glanced down towards the riverbank and spotted something. 'Oh, there she is, daydreaming as usual.'

Mandy smiled and stood up, took Henry's cage and headed quietly for the river, as Sonia turned her face to the sun, ready for a spot of sunbathing.

Mandy didn't say anything as she sat down beside Leanne, who just gazed at the water which swirled lazily at her feet. Instead, she took Henry from his cage and settled him on her own lap. She began to tickle his ears with a blade of grass and waited for her friend to respond. Eventually, Leanne's gaze swivelled sideways.

'Hi, Mandy. Hi, Henry.' Leanne's low voice ended in a sigh.

'Hi.' Mandy handed over the hamster. 'Don't you think he's lost weight? James's diet is working really well.' She was careful not to mention the episode with Justin and Vicki earlier that day.

Leanne drew Henry to eye level in the palm of her hand. She nestled him close against her cheek. 'Yes, and he's still so soft!'

'And his coat is really shiny now!' Mandy agreed. 'That's down to the exercise and a better diet. We cut out all the starchy snacks that the kids used to give him at school.'

Leanne sighed again. She handed Henry back to Mandy and drew her knees under her chin.

'I have to go home the day after tomorrow.'

'I know. Will you be glad?'

'In one way. I'm looking forward to seeing my mum. But I won't see Henry any more, will I?'

Mandy hesitated. 'You could come back and see him,' she offered. 'Whenever you want.'

But Leanne turned away. 'I don't think so, Mandy.'

'Oh, don't mind what some people round here are saying!' Mandy wanted to put the record straight. 'Take no notice of the likes of Justin and Vicki. Whatever they say, we think it's great having you here, me and James, that is. And my mum and dad, and my grandparents. And James's family. We all like having the caravans in the village!'

A brief smile flitted across Leanne's thin face. 'But you haven't heard the latest, have you?'

'No, what?' Mandy stroked Henry and put him in his cage for a rest.

'Well, you know the tennis courts?'

Mandy nodded. 'Just over there.' She pointed a couple of hundred metres up river.

'There's a few new trees planted along by the riverbank.'

'I know.' Mandy pictured the saplings, carefully supported by thick wooden stakes and protected by a slim plastic tube around their trunks.

'Well, someone went along and snapped two of them clean in half. For no reason. No one saw it happen, but guess who got the blame?' Leanne turned to Mandy, her eyes full of anger. 'No, you don't need to say it out loud!'

Mandy groaned. 'Not again!'

'See. Whatever goes wrong round here, we get the blame for it. And those twins enjoyed rubbing my nose in it, I can tell you!'

'This afternoon?'

Leanne nodded. 'I was just walking down to James's house when they saw me and stopped me. Then, when they found out where I was from, they started yelling and calling me names.'

'What did they say?' Mandy went to stand at the water's edge. She felt ashamed and angry at the same time.

'All sorts of things. They called us vandals and stuff like that. They said to get back to the city where we belonged. And they said everyone round here hates us!'

'Well, we don't!' Mandy was steadfast. She tried to think straight. 'Anything could've happened to those trees. Just like Walter's flowerpots! I'll go home and ask Grandad; he knows all about what happens down at the tennis courts!'

Leanne tried to smile. 'Thanks, Mandy. But it's too late.'

'No, it's not. We'll get to the bottom of what's going on around here,' she promised.

'I hope you do. But what I mean is, it's too late for us. Too late for me. I can't come back to Welford and visit, see. Not after a week like this. I wouldn't ever dare to show my face again!'

Mandy poked the toe of her trainer into the clear water. 'Do you all think like that? Marcie, Sonia, Paul, and the rest?'

'Pretty well. Look, it's not your fault. Just forget it, Mandy.' Leanne stood up and ran a hand through her red hair, pushing it clear of her face. 'I only hope the kids who come to Riverside after us get on better with the people in the village. Maybe it's just our bunch that they don't like.'

'I doubt it,' Mandy shook her head, thinking of the fuss that Mr Western, Mrs Ponsonby and Mrs Parker Smythe would be making over the latest 'proof' against the caravanners.

'Well.' Leanne shrugged and turned to go. Then she remembered Henry and stooped to peep into his cage. 'Bye, Henry,' she whispered.

Henry twitched his little nose and blinked. He ran to the front of his cage to peer back.

'Do you think he knows I'm saying goodbye?' Leanne asked as she turned away, her eyes brimming with tears.

Mandy couldn't bring herself to answer. She watched as Leanne walked off towards her caravan, her own eyes filling with tears at the sadness and injustice of it all.

Eight

'Not a very good day for a barbecue,' Gran commented when she dropped in on Animal Ark the following morning. The sky had turned cloudy overnight, and a soft drizzle had begun to fall.

'Not a very good day, full stop!' Mandy stood in reception. She was wearing her white vet's coat and an unusually downhearted expression. Surgery wasn't due to begin for half an hour, so Mandy was keeping herself busy by tidying Jean Knox's desk.

'Why, what's the matter?' Gran bustled up the steps and put her shopping basket on a chair in the waiting-room. 'This isn't like you, Mandy dear.' She smiled a greeting at her son, Adam Hope, already at work in one of the treatment rooms. He was getting Jemima ready to go home after the successful operation on her tail.

'Hello there, Mum.' He came out. 'What brings you here? I was going to say bright and early, but it isn't really, is it?'

'Apparently not.' Gran was puzzled by the dull atmosphere. She looked curiously at her son.

'No use rolling your eyes and raising your eyebrows, Mum.' Mandy's dad came out with it straight. 'Why don't you get Mandy to tell you the latest episode in the Riverside soap opera? It's on daily, you know. It looks like you missed the latest dramatic instalment!'

'Ah!' Gran seemed to see the light. 'You mean the broken trees? Oh yes, I heard about that. As a matter of fact, Tom is down at the tennis courts right this moment, taking a look.' To make herself useful, she joined Mandy at the desk and began to sort out leaflets about booster injections against cat flu and other common ailments.

When the phone rang, Gran quickly picked it up. 'It's for you,' she said to Mandy, handing it over. 'Your mum's put the call through from the house.'

'Hello?' Mandy wasn't expecting a call.

'Hello.' A small voice spoke, then hesitated. 'This is Imogen.'

'Hi, Imogen!' She tried to hide her surprise. 'There isn't something the matter with Button or Barney, is there?' She couldn't think why else Imogen Parker Smythe would want to get in touch.

'No, it's not that. It's just that I wanted to say I was sorry.'

'What about?' Mandy gave her gran a puzzled frown.

'About my mum writing off to the council people again with that long list of names.'

'The petition!' Mandy's voice rose. 'You mean they've actually sent it off?'

'This morning. Does that mean the caravans will have to leave?' Imogen sounded upset. 'People don't like the caravan children, do they?'

'Some people don't,' Mandy agreed. 'But thanks for telling me, Imogen.' There was another long pause. 'There isn't anything else, is there?' She suspected there was something else on Imogen's mind.

'No. Yes! That is, can you come to my house?' The trembling voice sounded tearful. 'I need to tell you something else; a secret. But I can't say it on the phone.'

'Oh right, I'll try to later on,' Mandy promised.

But her mind was on the petition. It seemed Mr Western, Mrs Ponsonby and Imogen's mum were really determined to get rid of the caravans at last. 'Bye then,' she said absent-mindedly, and she put the phone down.

'It looks like they're going to win,' she told her gran. 'I bet they've been collecting signatures all week. And now they'll say they've got proper evidence!'

Mr Hope snorted and retired to his treatment room. 'Evidence!'

'They will have told the council about the flowerpots, the cows on the loose up on the moorside, and now the broken trees,' Mandy continued. 'They'll say permission for the caravan site should be withdrawn because of all the trouble the city kids have caused.'

Gran's tongue tut-tutted rapidly. 'Well, really!'

'It's not fair, is it, Gran?'

'It certainly is not!' She tapped the sheaf of leaflets smartly against the desk. 'From what Tom says, it doesn't seem likely that even superhuman children could have broken those saplings. He says they were probably too strong to be snapped off like that.'

'Exactly!' Mandy agreed.

'That's why he wanted to take a look for himself.'

'Now, there's no point in you two just guessing,'

Mr Hope warned from the other room. 'That would make you as bad as Sam Western's lot!'

'No way!' Mandy was put out. 'This isn't *guessing*, Dad!' Her fighting spirit was on the mend after her chat with Gran. 'Take the flowerpots; anyone coming out of the pub could've got into their car and backed into them!'

'Without even realising.' Gran was ready to back her up. 'Look, dear, what you must do now is follow up these theories. If you really want to help your friends at the caravan site, that is.'

'You're right, Gran!' With her head high, and a determined look on her face, she went into the treatment room. 'Dad, you don't need me for surgery this morning, do you?'

'No. Jemima here is ready for Reverend Hadcroft to collect. And Simon's due at any moment. There aren't many appointments in the book, I don't think. Why?' His eyes twinkled at her.

'You know why! I want to go and see Grandad. Then I want to go up to Beacon House to see Imogen. I think she might have something important to tell me. Then after that, I don't know what I'll do. It depends how I get on.'

'Get on with what?' He played dumb, his head to one side.

'With my investigations! I intend to find out the real people behind all this damage!' she said in a strong clear voice. 'It's wrong for Riverside to get all the blame. It'll ruin everything for the kids who are supposed to come here for their holidays this summer.'

'That's my girl!' A smile spread across Mr Hope's face as he gave her a quick hug.

Mandy grinned back and took off her white coat. 'Thanks, Gran,' she said, as she hung it on its hook. And without waiting for any more advice, she ran outside for her bike and pedalled swiftly down to the tennis courts.

Grandad stood in the drizzle, hunched up in his green padded waistcoat. He stared thoughtfully at the two snapped saplings. The cruel, jagged ends showed up pale through the mist. He looked up as Mandy ran to greet him.

'Hello, where's your jacket, love?' he asked, casting an eye at the heavy clouds. 'And what brings you down here?'

'I was looking for you, Grandad.' She tramped through the long grass. Behind her, the immaculate grass courts stretched, smooth as snooker-tables. 'I wanted to know what you think. Did kids do this?'

She went and peered closely at the damaged trees.

Slowly Grandad shook his head. 'Do you want my expert opinion, love?'

She nodded eagerly. Her grandad knew everything there was to know about plants and gardening. He would know how hard it was to snap these trees.

'Well, I'd say it was impossible to do that with bare hands.'

Mandy took a sharp breath. 'Oh, Grandad!'

'I mean it. Just imagine, if you ever try to get rid of a strong shoot that you didn't want growing in your garden; a bramble or a stray sycamore. Well, it takes all your strength to snap something like that, and these two trees here are a good bit thicker than that.'

Mandy pushed a stray, wet strand of hair from her forehead. 'So what do you think could have done it?'

Grandad stooped to examine the ruined trunks. He sighed. 'That's harder to say. But look here, this plastic tube that protected the tree is split right down to the bottom, and there are scratches along the bark. I'd say that it was done by some sort of machine with sharp edges.' He stood up straight and looked up and down the riverbank, as if the machine could still be spotted there.

'A machine? What sort of machine?'

'Who knows? But if you think about it, it has to be a Land-rover, or a tractor or some such thing, to get down here. Yes, I'd say it was something strong and heavy like that. It must have caught the trees as it passed.'

'But definitely not kids?' she repeated.

'No,' he said. 'Definitely not.'

With fresh hope in her heart, Mandy waved goodbye to her grandad and shot off again on her bike in the direction of Beacon House. Grandad had promised to pass on his verdict to people in the village, while Mandy raced up to visit Imogen Parker Smythe.

'It may be too late to stop the petition now,' he warned. 'And there are those other incidents supposedly involving the Riverside children, remember!'

But Mandy refused to be cast down. As she cycled up the long hill, her legs aching, her chest heaving, she felt sure that this next visit would be another step towards clearing their name. After all, Imogen's phone call had come out of the blue. And she'd sounded shaky, as if something was bothering her.

Mandy arrived at last, found the security gates open and a black car standing in the drive. She cycled straight up to the front door of Beacon House, then rang the bell, glad to see Imogen's dad and not her mum come through the hall to answer it.

He opened the door. 'Hello,' Mr Parker Smythe said, surprised by Mandy's damp and dishevelled appearance. 'Have you come to see Immi?' He stood in a bright green golf sweater, one hand on the door, holding it half open. Imogen herself came bounding downstairs two at a time. 'Mandy's come to play!' she shouted, slipping in between her tall father and the door. 'I invited her!' She dragged Mandy by the arm into the tiled hallway and straight upstairs. At seven years old, she was small, but chubby and strong. Mandy felt herself being propelled into Imogen's splendid bedroom, complete with television, phone, shower-room and cuddly toys.

Quickly Imogen pushed the door closed. 'Oh good, you came!' she gasped, still refusing to let go of Mandy's arm.

Mandy stared at her red cheeks and secretive expression. 'Are you OK?' She felt herself plumped down on the embroidered white duvet on Imogen's soft bed. A giant black and white panda and a pink teddy bear toppled from the banked-up pillows and fell into her lap.

'Yes! No! Oh dear!' Imogen too collapsed on the bed, half in tears. 'I've got something to tell you, only Mummy will be cross with me if I do.' She bit her lip and turned away. 'I wish I'd told someone sooner, then they wouldn't have got into all this trouble!'

'Who? Who wouldn't have got into trouble?' Mandy tried to calm her down by speaking quietly.

'Those caravan children. They're going to be sent away, aren't they? The caravans, I mean. And all because of the flowerpots. And Mummy says they deserve it, and it's my fault because I let her think it was them, and then it was too late!' Imogen wailed and buried her face in her hands.

'Too late?' Mandy repeated. 'No, it's not too late, Imogen. You can tell me what really happened. You know, don't you?'

Miserably the little girl looked up and nodded. 'I saw. Mummy was in the post office buying a newspaper. I stayed in the car.' She paused.

'Go on,' Mandy said quietly. 'You see, it isn't fair to let someone take the blame when it's not their fault. You wouldn't like it, would you?'

Imogen shook her head. 'I never noticed the flowerpots at first. I was looking at the cat.'

'Which cat?'

'Mr Pickard's big tomcat. He was sitting on the wall in the sun.'

Mandy nodded. 'That must have been Tom. Then what?'

'Next thing, the little poodle came running up to him. She jumped up. Tom hissed, and the dog jumped higher and higher, till it crashed into a flowerpot. She sent them all crashing down. Tom ran off and the dog stopped barking. When Mummy came out of the shop, they'd both run away. All the flowers were on the ground and the pots were broken!'

Mandy took a deep breath. 'And your mum didn't notice there was anything wrong?'

Again Imogen shook her head.

'Do you know whose dog it was?'

'It was a little white dog with a red collar. They shouted out its name. They called her Antonia, but she never took any notice!'

'Who's they? Who called?' Mandy frowned. These unknown people had witnessed the accident along with Imogen, but they too had kept quiet about it ever since. She felt herself grow hot and angry.

'I don't know. It was a big girl and boy. They both looked the same. I think they must have been twins,' Imogen tailed off tearfully. 'Mummy drove away and

I never said anything because I thought the big boy and girl would get into trouble. And then . . . and then, everyone said it was the caravan children, and it was too late!' Imogen set about crying in earnest.

'Vicki and Justin Simpson!' Mandy let the truth sink in. Then she stood up, freeing herself from Imogen. She felt a small surge of victory; here was the first real proof that the Riverside children were innocent!

She went straight out and found Mr Parker Smythe still hovering at the bottom of the stairs. Mandy explained why Imogen was upset. He listened and nodded, then quickly took charge.

'I don't know much about this petition,' he confessed. 'I've been away on business for most of this week. But from what you say, it seems I'd better tell my wife what really happened to the flowerpots. It puts a whole new light on things. Leave it to me. I'll see what I can do,' he promised.

'Will you please tell Mr Western and Mrs Ponsonby too?' Mandy felt that things were working out well. Now she longed to race down to Riverside and tell them about the progress they'd made; the city visitors were in the clear over breaking the flowerpots and the trees.

'Of course.' He nodded kindly.

'And tell Imogen thanks from me, would you?' Mandy headed for the door. 'And ask her if she'd like to come to the barbecue this evening. She can come and join in the celebrations, all being well!'

Then she was off, down the long drive under the oak trees. She jumped on her bike, sped down the twisting road, through the village as the clouds began to lift and a watery sun shone through. She raced along the lane to the Hunters' house, brimming with excitement, hardly able to contain the good news. 'James will want to come with me!' she told herself firmly, flinging open his garden gate.

'James!' She ran up the path. The house was shut up. There was no car in the drive. Even Blackie was silent. Only Eric stalked across the lawn, his tail up and swishing from side to side.

That's odd, Mandy thought, halting in mid-stride. She spotted yellow flower-heads lying scattered over the grass, and one of Mr Hunter's flower-beds had been roughly trampled. Crushed marigolds lay on the damp soil, their petals strewn far and wide.

'James!' Now Mandy ran down the side of the house, to see if anyone was there. But the doors and windows were shut. Everyone was out and alarm began to dart through her. Who had come in and trampled on the garden? Was anything else damaged? She flew back round the front of the house and stared at the lawn, then slowly she went up the bottom step into the front porch.

'Henry?' Her voice caught in her dry throat. There was the cage on the shelf. But the top was flung open. 'Oh no!' She leaped the final two steps to look inside the cage. Henry's straw bedding was scattered loosely over the bottom, his drinking bowl had been tipped over, the sawdust was waterlogged. Even his exercise wheel lay on one side, and the ramp to his sleeping gallery had been wrenched out of position. 'Oh, Henry!' Mandy gasped. Frantically she searched every corner. But it was no good; the hamster's cage was empty. Henry had vanished.

Nine

'And you're sure you left the cage safely locked?' Mrs Hunter repeated. She stood in the porch, trying to understand what was going on.

James was white-faced. They'd searched long and hard for Henry since they'd arrived home from shopping, but now he stood and stared at the empty cage. 'Yes, I locked him in! I'm sure I did!'

'Yes, look, the lock's been forced open,' Mandy said. She examined the twisted bolt. 'It's not James's fault, Mrs Hunter. Henry didn't just escape. He's been stolen!'

James's mother put down her shopping and went to let Blackie out of the back of the car. The dog bounded up the steps and began to sniff around the porch. He gave a sharp bark. Then his head went down again as he trotted out on to the lawn.

'I think he's picked up some sort of scent.' Mandy tried to think straight. James's car had arrived just as she'd discovered Henry's disappearance. She had greeted them with the dreadful news and watched the colour drain from her friend's face. 'Blackie knows there's been an intruder, don't you, boy?' She had followed him into the garden, as the dog sniffed among the scattered marigold petals and the deep footprints in the flowerbed.

'But why? What's going on?' James sat heavily on the top step of the porch. He fought to control his feelings. 'Mandy, what am I going to tell Miss Temple when we get back to school? I can't tell her that I lost Henry, can I?'

'You didn't,' Mandy said firmly. 'Henry's been taken deliberately. Whoever stole Henry made a mess of the garden as well. Now, why would anyone want to do that?' She went to where the Labrador was sniffing at the deep prints. But her thoughts whirled without order. Henry was missing. The cage was empty. The flowers were trampled. But none of it came together to make any sense.

'And that's not the only thing.' Mrs Hunter sighed

as she swung down the back door of the car. 'We just drove through the village on the way back from the supermarket. There was a bit of a kerfuffle going on outside the pub. We stopped to find out what it was about. Apparently one of the kids from the caravan site is missing. Pete Cavendish was there trying to organise a sort of search party.'

James sat with his head in his hands, not reacting. But Mandy felt the hairs on the back of her neck start to prickle at the news. 'Who? Who's gone missing?' This was the last day at Riverside for the Kingsmill children. Everyone should be getting ready for tonight's barbecue, not spending time searching for one of their party.

'I don't remember the name,' Mrs Hunter eased past James to take her shopping into the house. 'Do you?' she asked him. 'James, Mandy was asking who they're looking for in the village.'

James looked up. 'Leanne,' he said quietly.

'I knew it!'

'She went off some time this morning and she's not been seen for hours. No one saw where she went.'

'Oh no!' The prickling sensation spread down her spine. 'Oh James, you don't think Leanne . . . she can't have, can she?' Mandy stared over his head at Henry's empty cage.

'You mean, Leanne was feeling so bad about leaving tomorrow and not seeing Henry again, and she was so fed-up and miserable about everything that she came and stole him and ran away?'

Mandy nodded. 'I'm not saying she *did*! I'm just saying she *might have*!' If you added things up, it was quite possible. She groaned. 'Why couldn't she just have waited an hour or two longer?'

Still shocked by Henry's disappearance, James got slowly to his feet. 'Why, what difference would that have made?'

'We could have got over to Riverside and told them the latest news. It turns out the Kingsmill kids had nothing to do with Walter's flowerpots getting smashed, and probably nothing to do with the broken trees either!' Rushing through the morning's events, Mandy told James what had really gone on. 'If Leanne had known that and knew that people in the village might not be so horrible to her any more, surely she would never have run off like this!'

'Maybe.' Mrs Hunter came out of the house with two cups of tea. She handed one to James. 'Here, I think you should drink this while I telephone your father at work. I want to discuss what we should do. I've already checked inside the house, and everything there is just as we left it. It's only the garden that's damaged, and of course, poor Henry.'

She left them to mope over the defenceless little hamster; short-sighted, over-friendly Henry, with his lovely marmalade coat and twitching whiskers. Where was he now? Was somebody taking good care of him? Mandy shuddered at the thought that the kidnapper might take fright and abandon him. He could be stranded in the middle of nowhere, unable to look after himself, and terrified.

'I only hope Leanne is looking after him,' James said miserably. His own thoughts had tended in the same direction.

'Oh, she will!' Mandy put on a brave face. 'Leanne *loves* Henry!'

'If it *was* Leanne.'

'Well, they both seem to have gone missing at more or less the same time. And she knew she was never going to see Henry again; she told me she'd never come back to Welford.'

There was a pause. They were at a loss, still swamped by fears for the missing hamster.

Then Mrs Hunter came bustling back. 'I phoned your dad, James. He says not to worry. We could always buy another hamster for the school.'

He shook his head. 'It wouldn't be the same.'

'No, but your dad was only trying to be practical. For instance, he wondered what was the point of the intruder trampling through the flowerbed. I must say, I find that very strange too!'

They all wandered across the lawn together to examine the heavy footprints.

'Well, it was no accident, that's for sure,' Mandy said. 'Someone's great big boots have stamped over here on purpose.'

'Your dad also said that if this Leanne girl is your prime suspect for Henry-napping, why don't you two go and join in the search for her? Better than standing around doing nothing.'

It took Mandy only a second to agree. 'Let's take Blackie,' she suggested. 'I'm sure he's picked up the scent. If we take him along, he can help in the search!'

So they went off down the lane, with Blackie eagerly snuffling and tracking a scent. They approached Chrissie Searle, standing at the entrance to the caravan site. She was poring over an ordnance survey map and directing Marcie and Sonia towards the wood where Leanne sometimes hung out.

She greeted them with a worried frown. 'Have you heard?'

Mandy nodded. 'We've come to help you look.' She thought it best to keep their suspicions about Leanne and Henry to themselves.

'That's good of you, thanks.' Chrissie sighed. 'Poor kid, I think she's been really unhappy here.'

'What do you want us to do?' James asked. He had to restrain Blackie by putting him on a short lead. 'Follow the others?'

'No, I've got this side of the village more or less covered. There's no real panic just yet. She's only been gone a couple of hours. But Marcie overheard her crying late last night, and this morning no one could get a word out of her at breakfast. Then she went missing. Pete and I thought it would be as well to start checking things out. We've been worried about her all along. She was too much of a loner, and now it looks as if something was really bothering her.'

Mandy nodded. She turned to James. 'Let's run on to the village, to see if there's anything we can do there.'

'Good idea.' Chrissie folded up her map, ready to set off up the hill after the distant figures of Ben and Paul. 'You'll find Pete organising things there. Half the village has turned out to help, much to our surprise!' With a nod, she set off along the public footpath, peering carefully to right and left as she went.

Mandy was surprised to see Mrs Ponsonby, brightly dressed in a daffodil-yellow outfit. She was at the centre of the huddle of people gathered outside the Fox and Goose, standing beside the tall figure of Mr Parker Smythe. Pete Cavendish, Mrs Platt, Walter Pickard and Ernie Bell were also listening closely.

As Mandy and James approached, they heard Mrs Ponsonby begin to hold forth.

'. . . So it seems, Walter, we may have been wrong all along!' Her rich voice rose above the murmur of all the rest. 'Most unfortunate, but all too true, I'm afraid!'

Mandy stopped and stared at James.

'Sit, Blackie!' he ordered quietly. In spite of their worries about Leanne and Henry, the opportunity to hear Mrs Ponsonby launching into a full apology was too good to miss. They hovered quietly by the side of the pub.

'If, as Mr Parker Smythe says, there are eye witnesses!' Mrs Ponsonby considered things. 'And of course, Mr Parker Smythe, we would never doubt your word. No indeed! We know very well that you always have the best interests of the village at heart!' She flattered and smiled, holding Pandora snuggled under one arm, with patient Toby sitting to heel amongst the crush of trouser-legs and skirts.

'And I'm sorry to hear that naughty Antonia and Tom were the ones who were to blame,' Mrs Ponsonby continued. 'You see, Walter,' there was a teenie-weenie fight between them, and your poor geraniums became the casualties of war! A pure accident, of course. I know that little Antonia can be a teenie bit wild at times, can't she, Pandora? But I'm sure she didn't mean any real harm!'

Walter stood in his shirt-sleeves, scratching his head. 'Aye well, Tom's always up to mischief. And he's never been one to back away from a fight.'

Mandy peered round the corner to hear Mrs Platt offer her own, much quieter apology. 'If I'd known Antonia had had anything to do with it, or that nephew and niece of mine, I'd have been straight up the street, knocking on your door with the money to pay for the new plants,' she assured him. 'I'm very sorry, Walter. I really am.'

'Aye well,' Walter mumbled again. 'It's all water under the bridge.' He took a glance at his bare wall and shook his head.

In the short silence that followed, Mandy, James

and Blackie went forward to join the group. By now Mrs Ponsonby was gathering fresh steam. She fixed her straw hat firmly on her head and made a solemn announcement. 'The truth is out, and all thanks to Mr Parker Smythe's dear little girl, Imogen! And we have to be big enough to admit, each and every one of us, that we made a terrible mistake in making out that the caravan children were the cause of it all!'

'Blow me down!' Ernie Bell muttered. He gave a sly wink as he spotted Mandy.

'No!' Mrs Ponsonby raised her free hand to beg for silence. 'We must! Mr Western, Mrs Parker Smythe and I simply jumped to the wrong conclusion. And I know I speak for them all when I say that we wish to make amends!'

She turned with a swish of yellow skirt to face Pete Cavendish. 'To show how truly sorry we are, I can pledge that the whole village will stand by on the alert to help you in your search for the unfortunate girl. It seems she's a sensitive little soul, and our accusations may well have pushed her to the very brink before she decided to run away!' Mrs Ponsonby's voice had taken on a low, sorrowful tone. 'The very least we can do is to help to find her!'

Pete Cavendish nodded his dark, wavy head. 'Thanks very much, Mrs Ponsonby.'

'Not at all. Now, first we need a description!'

'Well, Leanne is fairly small and slim. She has chin length, red hair; lots of it, and she was wearing a blue and white T-shirt, jeans and trainers.' Pete filled them in on the appearance of the missing girl.

'Very good.' Mrs Ponsonby squared her shoulders. 'Pass that round, everybody! Now I must go and telephone Mr Western to inform him of the latest position. Ernie, you come along with me to Bleakfell Hall. We must make a thorough search of the grounds, leave no stone unturned. Come along now, everyone!'

Mandy and James watched poor Ernie's face fall a mile. But there was no arguing with Mrs Ponsonby. They watched the group disperse. Mr Parker Smythe promised to check the moortop beyond Beacon House, while Walter wandered off towards the pub to rustle up more help.

'We'll head down the valley,' Mandy told Pete. 'I know Leanne didn't usually go down that way, towards Greystones Farm, but all the more reason for looking down there, I suppose.'

'You may well be right.' Pete nodded his approval.

'Aren't you going to call the police?' James asked. He still had Blackie on the lead. The dog seemed upset by recent events, and was being even more disobedient that usual. He was whining and straining to be off the leash.

'Not yet. If Leanne hasn't turned up by teatime, we'll think again. But I'd like to make a thorough search ourselves before involving anyone else. We don't want to be alarmist; in the end we might find that she just wandered off for a quiet stroll. You know what she's like.' But though he sounded calm, he looked worried. 'Go on, you look down river, like you said. We'll all meet up again at four, back at Riverside. OK?'

Mandy and James nodded and set off. Now James could let Blackie off the lead, and he streaked ahead, down the path by Walter's cottage, towards the river. They could just see his black tail waving above the tall grass. 'He seems to know where we're heading!' Mandy said. They had to run to keep him in sight. 'Look, he's picking up that scent again!'

'This way, that's right, boy!' James said. They took a left turn by the edge of the clear water, and headed for the square stone farmhouse in the distance where Brandon Gill and his family ran their pig farm. Blackie sniffed and was off again, loping along the pebbly shore, while Mandy and James kept to the narrow path.

Mandy seized a long stick from the bank and used it to swish aside bushes and undergrowth of poor-man's-orchid and willowherb. A strong aniseed perfume rose in the damp air.

'At least it's stopped raining,' James said. 'That's something, I suppose.' Then he drew to a sudden halt. 'Shh! Here, Blackie! Here, boy!'

Mandy halted too, while the dog charged ahead regardless. 'What is it?'

'I spotted something.' James crouched and peered through some bushes towards a clearing about fifty metres ahead.

'Yes!' Mandy saw a patch of blue, then red. 'Two people!' She saw Blackie race into the clearing, barking frantically. She stood up and sighed. 'Well, no chance of sneaking up on them, whoever it is. What's got into Blackie? I've never seen him as disobedient as this!'

James shook his head. They heard a boy's voice call. 'All right, James Hunter, we know you're there! Come out, come out, wherever you are!' The voice mocked them. Mandy recognised the jeering tone of Justin Simpson.

'Oh no!' This was the last person she wanted to meet.

'Can't you keep your dog under control?'

he taunted, as James and Mandy emerged into the clearing.

'You can talk!' Mandy retorted. She felt herself colour up, as she mumbled a quick hello to Brandon and confronted Justin. It was Justin's red shirt that she'd spotted, and he stood now, swinging his foot at Blackie, who had crouched, alert and growling, just out of reach.

'What are you on about?' Justin hooked his thumbs into his belt and tried to outstare Mandy.

'I mean, you can't even keep your aunt's poodle under control!' she said angrily. She hated to see anyone trying to use their feet against an animal.

He realised in a flash what she meant, and turned to avoid her gaze. 'Who told you about that?'

'Never mind. But we know it was you and Vicki who let Antonia have that scrap with old Tom. Those flowerpots were down to you two!'

'Says who?' Justin bluffed, then resorted to insult. 'You're a right pair of little detectives, aren't you?' he sneered.

'Now hang on a minute,' Brandon cut in. 'No need to be nasty, Justin!' He looked puzzled. 'What's up with Blackie, James? He isn't usually like this.'

The dog had crouched low, ready to leap forward at James's command. He growled and glared at Justin.

But now Mandy stopped dead in her tracks. She forgot the flowerpots. She forgot Antonia and Tom. Her mind was focused on something completely new. 'Trainers!' she said in a faint whisper.

'What?' James held on to Blackie's collar and tried to calm him. 'What on earth are you on about, Mandy?'

'Trainers! Remember, Pete said Leanne was wearing a blue and white top, jeans and *trainers*!'

'So?' James held on tight to Blackie. Justin stood his ground, feet planted wide apart, while Brandon frowned in bewilderment.

'It wasn't trainers that made those footprints in your garden, James! It was a pair of heavy boots!' She stared at Justin's feet. That was what had done it; she'd noticed the mud caked to his black boots as he swung out at Blackie. 'It wasn't Leanne after all!'

The sound of her voice, breathless and scared, set Blackie off again. He barked and strained against James, snarling at Justin, who still braved it out. Behind the bravado, Mandy thought she saw a flicker of real fear.

'Just what are you trying to prove?' Justin demanded. He laughed and jerked his head back in contempt.

But Mandy's mind was made up. Justin was mixed up in this somehow. That was why Blackie had flown at him; the dog had followed his scent all the way from the garden to this clearing. Justin Simpson was the one who'd trampled the flowers. And there was mud on the patterned sole of his heavy boots to prove it.

'Where's Vicki, Justin?' she whispered. Her gaze flicked sideways to the gnarled and twisted trunks of the hawthorns at the far side of the clearing.

'Not here. Why?'

If Justin was involved, Vicki was seldom far away.

Mandy turned to stare at him again through narrowed eyes.

'OK. So where's Henry?' She met his angry gaze. She managed to speak calmly.

Justin snorted then laughed. 'Are you crazy? That's it, you're round the bend, Mandy Hope!' He lunged at her, but Brandon held him off.

'Steady on!'

Justin wrenched free. 'Lay off, Brandon! Keep out of this! And you'd better not go spreading rumours about me and my sister!' he yelled at Mandy. 'You can't prove a thing, and I'll say you're round the twist! I'll say you set that dog on to me, Hunter! I'll tell everyone it's mad and dangerous!' Justin glared as he backed off from Blackie. Then he bent to seize a rough stone the size of his fist. He flung it at Blackie, missing his head by centimetres.

This time, Brandon flung himself at the dog to stop him from launching himself at the enemy. '*You're* the mad idiot round here!' he yelled at Justin.

Justin laughed as he scrambled up the bank between the trees. Then he vaulted a wall, out of sight.

'Quick!' Mandy ran and grabbed James by the arm. 'Come on, you two,' she said. 'We've got to find Vicki before he does!'

'Why? What's going on round here?' Brandon demanded. He stroked Blackie's soft black nose to calm him down.

'Vicki's the one who took Henry!' Mandy cried. 'I'm certain of it! Come on, you two, let's try Mrs Platt's house. We've got to get there first, or who knows what they'll do to him!'

Ten

'Yes,' Mrs Platt admitted. Her face was creased into a worried frown. 'Yes, as a matter of fact, I think Vicki did have a little hamster in her room. I couldn't think where it had come from, but before I could ask her about it, Justin came back home!'

Mandy stood on the doorstep of Mrs Platt's small, neat bungalow, nodding breathlessly. 'When was that, Mrs Platt? Can you tell me how long ago Justin arrived?'

The twins' mild-mannered great-aunt thought for a moment that seemed to stretch to an age. *Please be quick*, Mandy thought. She had more questions jostling for position as she waited for Mrs Platt's reply.

'Not long ago. A few minutes, that's all. It seemed as if he was in an almighty hurry, banging doors and charging about.'

'And you say that he and Vicki went straight out again?'

'Yes. He dashed into her room with something urgent to tell her, I expect. Before I had time to turn round they were both racing out of the front door. I could hear Antonia barking out in the street. They didn't even bother to fasten the front gate!'

'Did Vicki take Henry, I mean, the hamster, with her? Did you notice?'

Again Mrs Platt nodded, then frowned. 'Oh dear, I'm afraid they've got themselves into more trouble, haven't they?'

Mandy didn't reply. Justin had beaten them to it after all. He must have cut across country from Brandon's place, across the farmers' fields, to reach the village before them. 'Do you know where they were going, Mrs Platt?'

'Oh no, dear. They didn't tell me. They were in far too much of a hurry.' Mrs Platt kept an eye on Antonia, who trotted down the path to greet Blackie. James and Brandon were waiting with him at the gate. Suddenly, she looked at them aghast. 'You don't mean to say that you think Vicki *stole* the hamster? Oh, surely not!'

Mandy nodded. 'That's what it looks like. Did you see which way they went?' By now, her heart was in her mouth. Justin must have told Vicki that they'd been found out. Now they were both out there with Henry, and probably about to do something desperate.

'Oh dear, now wait a minute. Yes, they went that way!' Mrs Platt waved her hand towards the main street, past the pub and the church, towards Riverside. 'When I went out to fetch Antonia back in I spotted them heading up the lane towards the caravan site!'

'Thanks!' Mandy gasped. She turned and ran down the path. 'They're heading for Riverside!' she told James and Brandon. 'And they've got Henry! Come on, we'd better hurry!'

Straining every muscle to catch up with the culprits, the three of them raced the length of the village street. James let Blackie run ahead. When he came to the sign for Riverside, the Labrador darted sideways through the gate.

'That's it, good boy!' James cried. 'Where are they, Blackie? Go on, boy, fetch!'

Eager as ever, Blackie wove between the smart new caravans. The site looked deserted; everyone was out combing the area, looking for Leanne, so Blackie's busy nose wasn't distracted by other scents.

'Why would the twins head this way?' Brandon wondered. He paused to catch his breath just outside the camp shop.

James bent forward to ease a stitch in his side. 'I don't know. But you can bet your life that Blackie knows what he's doing. They've got to be round here somewhere!'

Meanwhile, Mandy went ahead, following on Blackie's heels, praying that he was on the right track. 'Go on, boy, find them!' She dropped on to her hands and knees to peer into the gloom under one of the caravans, then she backed out. Blackie had squeezed through to the other side and was off again, nose to the ground, tail wagging urgently for her to follow.

She ran clear of the caravans towards the longer grass by the riverbank. Blackie looked back and gave a short, sharp bark. He stood, ears pricked, hackles raised down the length of his spine. 'What is it?' She ran up to him. He crouched down and barked again, ran two or three steps, then returned.

'Show me, Blackie! Go on, boy!' Mandy whispered. She followed the dog down the bank on to the narrow pebble beach. And there Vicki was, crouching behind a tree branch that swept low over the water. She looked wretched and afraid.

'Keep him off me, Mandy! Don't let him bite!' she pleaded. Heavy strands of hair had fallen over her eyes, but Mandy could see how miserable she looked behind the tumbled locks. She gripped the bough until her knuckles turned white.

Mandy stared. 'It's all right, he won't hurt you,' she said. She stretched out both her hands and spoke carefully. 'Vicki, for heaven's sake, give Henry to me!'

Tears began to roll down the girl's face. 'I can't.' She trembled and hid her face behind her hands. 'I haven't got him!'

Mandy groaned. She heard Brandon and James running through the long grass. They came to a halt just a few metres behind. 'You must have, Vicki. Your aunt told us that you'd got him. Now just hand him over, please!' She felt her nerves stretch to their limit. Her own hands were trembling.

'No, honestly, I haven't got him any more!' She looked up and sniffed, trying to pull herself together. 'But it's all right, don't worry. Everything's going to be fine!'

Bewildered, Mandy glanced the length of the beach. 'What do you mean? Where is he? What have you done with Henry, Vicki?'

'Listen, I want to tell you the whole thing!' Vicki took a step forward. 'Tell him to sit, James.' She waited while Blackie obeyed his owner's command. Then she came up close to Mandy. 'All this happened because I was jealous,' she began. 'When James was allowed to bring Henry home for the summer, I didn't think it was fair!'

Mandy clearly remembered Vicki's mutterings and dark looks, but she was impatient. 'Vicki, we don't have time for this! Just tell us where Henry is now!'

'I will, Mandy. But first, I want you to listen. You have to understand, then you can tell everyone what happened. I don't want them to hate me after all this!'

Though Vicki was tall and easily able to take care of herself, something about the way she talked got through to Mandy. 'Look, it's OK. If we get Henry back safe and sound, none of this will matter,' Mandy assured her.

'Well, he's all right. You've got to believe me!'

Mandy nodded. 'Go on, then.'

'It's just that I've always wanted to take Henry home, see. And when James was the one who was chosen, I just thought it was so unfair. James and you have loads of animals to look after already.

'Anyway, I sat around at home moping and getting

on Justin's nerves. Then when we came to stay in Welford with my aunt, he had an idea!' By now, Vicki was so keen to tell her version of events that she forgot all about her fear of Blackie. She laid one hand on Mandy's arm. 'We were busy keeping out of trouble after Antonia knocked over those flowerpots. There isn't much to do in Welford, just hang around, you know. Then Justin had this idea! "Let's kidnap Henry, if you're so keen on looking after him!" he said. He thought it would stop me moaning and give us something to do.

'His other idea was to make it look like the kids from Riverside were the ones to blame again. He said it worked pretty well before. I asked how and he said, "Easy-peasy. We'll go over to James's place and make a bit of a mess of his garden, make it look like vandals have been at it again. Then all you have to do is nick Henry from his cage!" He said no one would ever know it was us!'

'And you went along with it?' Mandy stared at her, open-mouthed.

Vicki's lip trembled and she nodded. 'I just wanted to look after Henry!' she whispered.

James came and broke into the amazed silence. 'Go on, Vicki. Never mind the garden. Just tell us what happened next.'

'Well, the thing is, Justin went a bit mad. He trampled everywhere, I couldn't stop him. He said he had to make it look like the Riverside lot had been at it again.' The tears rose again as she looked at James. 'I'm really sorry, James!'

He nodded. 'Is that it? You wrecked the flowers and forced open Henry's cage?'

'No.' Vicki took another deep breath. 'It gets worse!'

'Go on, you might as well spit it out.' Brandon climbed down the bank and offered his common sense opinion. 'Get it over and done with.'

'It's about Leanne, isn't it?' Mandy took a guess. Somewhere in the middle of all this, she felt that Vicki would be able to explain Leanne's disappearance too.

'How did you know?'

'Well, she's gone missing, and my guess is she didn't vanish for nothing. Go on, Vicki, tell us what happened next.'

'I was just lifting Henry out of his cage. Justin broke open the bolt with a screwdriver he brought with him. I thought we were going to get clean away, but just then the gate swung open and it was Leanne walking up the path towards us. You should've seen her face, Mandy. It was like someone had shot her. She saw me holding Henry and she sort of gasped. She dropped a little bag of food she'd brought for him and she turned white as a sheet. She tried to grab Henry from me, but Justin got in the way and warned her to keep her mouth shut!'

Mandy pictured the scene; Leanne struggling to rescue Henry, Justin bullying. Two against one. No chance.

'Justin laughed at her. He said he'd put the blame on her when they found Henry missing! Everyone would know it was her because she was the one who was mad on Henry. He said everyone hated her anyway!'

Mandy's brows knitted together in a deep frown. 'What did she do?'

'She kind of crumpled, then she ran off. I just stood there. Justin thought it was funny, and he went off as if nothing had happened.' Vicki's voice trailed off at last.

'You know that Leanne's not been seen since, don't you?' James said quietly.

Miserably Vicki nodded. Her lip quivered again. 'I said I was sorry.'

Mandy wasn't sure that 'sorry' was enough. Leanne and Henry had both got the fright of their lives because of the twins, and they were both still missing. 'But you told me Henry was OK, didn't you? So just take us to him now.' She knew she sounded stiff and unfriendly, but right then she couldn't help it.

'OK, I'll show you. Come on.' Vicki led the way up the bank and through the caravan park. 'I did know that we'd done something really awful,' she confessed. 'When Justin showed up at Aunty's house, I said I wanted to take Henry straight back. That was after I'd had the chance to think about it. He was ever so mad. He said the plan had gone wrong in any case, and you'd found out the truth. I said I didn't care any more. I just wanted to put Henry back in his cage. I never wanted any of this to happen!'

'Is that where Justin is now, at my house?' James asked. He had Blackie back on the lead as they broke into a run across the field.

'Yes. In the end he had to agree.' Vicki began to gasp as she ran. 'But he said he would be the one to take Henry back. I'd only mess things up if I went along. He told me to wait here while he did it. He promised no one would see him if he was by himself.'

Mandy glanced at James. She didn't like the thought of Henry in Justin's tender care. 'Is your mum in?' she asked.

James nodded.

'But Justin would be able to creep up without

being seen, wouldn't he? He promised he would!' Vicki insisted.

'Let's hope.' Brandon pulled up as he reached the gate ahead of the others. He pointed across the road. 'Here comes Justin now.'

They heard Justin's heavy footsteps on the tarmac. They saw him bend and shove something quickly into the hedge. They waited as he stood up and looked around. Then he spotted them. His face fell a mile. Mandy went to meet him.

'It's OK. Vicki's told us the whole thing,' she said to him. 'It doesn't matter, just as long as Henry's back where he belongs!' She longed for him to confirm it; that Henry was snug in his cage. Just those words, that was all.

He rocked back on his heels, scowling. He gave a short laugh. 'Tough!' he said.

'What do you mean?' Vicki pushed forward. 'Justin, you promised to put Henry back!'

'Too risky,' he shrugged. 'There was someone in the house. I couldn't get anywhere near without being spotted.'

'What are you saying?' Mandy demanded. 'Where's Henry? What have you done with him?' She still hoped against hope that Justin had taken the hamster back. 'Where is he?'

'How should I know?'

'Why, what have you done with him?'

Justin coloured up, but he hid his guilt with a final show of bravado. 'Didn't you see? I just dumped him in the hedge back there.' He jerked one thumb over his shoulder. 'So what's wrong with that, then? I did him a favour, didn't I? No more treadling around on that old wheel for Henry. No more being locked up in a cage. I put him back in the wild. I set him free!'

Eleven

Terrified, Mandy ran along the lane. Setting Henry 'free' was like passing a death sentence. He would be in immediate danger from foxes, badgers, dogs, cats. Even the stress of being alone in a wide open space might be enough to kill him. She stooped to rummage through the undergrowth in the hedge bottom, hoping that he'd simply curled into a ball until they came to rescue him. But there was no sign.

'At least we know he's still in there somewhere,' James said. 'He can't have run out on to the road, or else we'd have seen him!'

She nodded. 'OK, let's all go back into the field

and spread out to look for him!' She turned to Vicki. 'Will you help? We need as many people as possible. Henry won't last very long if we leave him to fend for himself!'

Vicki glanced at Justin, whose face was by now red with shame. He hung his head forward and shifted uneasily from foot to foot. 'Yes, we'll help!' she said firmly. 'It's the least we can do. Come on, Justin, you stand guard out here in the road. Let's get a move on!' And she led the little band of searchers back into the field.

They looked high and low. They searched under clumps of grass and inside hollows. They combed the field, they called his name. Brandon delved into his pockets and found biscuit crumbs. They tried to tempt Henry out of his hiding place by scattering them along the hedgerow. All in vain.

Then they enlisted help, as some of the others drifted back to Riverside. The unsuccessful search for Leanne turned into a search for Henry; soon half the kids from Riverside were ferreting through the undergrowth, underneath caravans and down the riverbank.

But by four o'clock, Mandy's hopes of finding the hamster were sinking low.

'He can't just vanish!' Vicki protested.

They gathered in a knot outside the clubhouse; Mandy, James, Brandon, Justin and Vicki, while the Riverside crowd kept on looking. Chrissie Searle had just turned up from the village shop with a hamper full of bread rolls which she'd ordered for the barbecue. She reported that there was still no sign of Leanne.

'Let's think; what would Henry be most likely to do in a situation like this?' It was James who thought straight as usual.

'He'd build a nest!' Mandy said. 'That's what he'd try to do. He'd look for dry grass, bits of sheep's wool, anything soft. He'd want a nice warm place, somewhere out of the wind.' She tried to plot Henry's probable movements since Justin had dumped him in the hedge.

'Now, now, we mustn't stand round idly chatting!' A loud voice interrupted them. 'Don't you know that the poor girl is still missing?' A bright yellow figure strode across the field towards them.

Mandy stifled a groan. 'Leanne's not the only one, Mrs Ponsonby.' Quickly she told the newcomer about Henry.

'Well, let's not waste any more time!' Mrs Ponsonby rose to the occasion with true wartime spirit. She rallied the troops. 'Twins, you take Brandon with you and carry out a systematic search inside the caravans! Who's to say that Henry, like any sensible little hamster, hasn't taken refuge inside a nice warm sleeping-bag or sock drawer?'

Eagerly Mandy nodded. 'Yes, we haven't tried inside the caravans yet!'

So Brandon and the twins set off under Mrs Ponsonby's command. Next she turned to Mandy, James and Blackie, the light of determination glinting in her eyes. 'And have you tried inside the shop? Just the place for a hungry hamster, don't you think?'

She took a few steps towards the door. 'Now, while you continue with the search in here, let me see how I can make myself more useful!' She rolled up the chiffon sleeves of her yellow dress, then turned to Chrissie Searle. 'Chrissie, my dear, I take it that the hamper contains provisions for tonight's barbecue?' Mrs Ponsonby didn't pause for a reply. 'Well, just carry it inside for me, would you, dear? My best plan is to press on with the food preparations, so that your little farewell party can go ahead according to schedule.' She marched inside with an air of hope and certainty.

Mandy's eyes widened. 'Do as she says!' she whispered. Chrissie picked up the hamper and turned after Mrs Ponsonby into the clubroom, while James and Mandy turned into the shop section, stacked with tins, boxes of crisps, shelves of biscuits and racks of fresh fruit.

'Isn't she amazing?' Chrissie said, once she'd deposited the hamper with Mrs Ponsonby, who straight away set to work with the bread knife. She sliced through the bread rolls with surgical precision. 'How can she be so sure we'll have anything to celebrate?'

'I don't know, but don't argue,' Mandy whispered. She dived behind the shop counter on her hands and knees, calling out Henry's name. Mrs Ponsonby had an eye on them through the open doorway. 'What are you going to do now?' Mandy asked Chrissie.

'Find Pete and carry on looking for Leanne. It may be time we got the police involved.' She looked serious as she went out and strode across the field.

Mrs Ponsonby had injected fresh energy into both searches. James stood on a chair to investigate the high shelves, while Mandy covered every square centimetre of the shop at ground level. Outside, the Riverside crowd still raked through the grass, while Vicki, Justin and Brandon carried on examining the caravans. But still there was no sign of Henry or Leanne.

Swish went the blade of Mrs Ponsonby's knife, chopping down on to the cutting-board. She used the snooker table covered with a sheet of thick plastic as a temporary surface. The bread rolls piled high on the table, as she lifted each one from the hamper to dissect it.

Swish – chop – pause. Swish – chop – pause.

'Henry!' Mandy called softly, trying to entice him out of hiding, crawling on all fours.

'Not up here,' James sighed. He climbed down from the chair.

'*Aagh!*' A scream rang out from Mrs Ponsonby. She snatched her hand away from the hamper, she dropped her knife and jumped a mile. 'Oh my, oh my! There's a rat!' She backed against the snooker table. 'In the hamper! A rat! Oh my, don't let it get out!'

Mandy and James sprang through the door into the clubroom. They spotted stout Mrs Ponsonby cowering against the table, her face and neck mottled red, her hands clasped in front of her chest. Together they dived for the hamper. They peered inside.

'It's not a rat; it's Henry!' James said calmly.

Mandy cried out in delight. 'Henry!' Unmistakably him, with his cheeks full of breadcrumbs, his thick golden coat dusted with flour, his eyes twinkling.

'No, no, it's a rat, a rodent! In the hamper! I'm sure it's a rat!' Mrs Ponsonby's chins quivered. Her wartime spirit had evaporated.

'No, look,' James explained, as Mandy gently lifted Henry from the hamper to cradle him in her hands. 'It's a hamster. He has no tail, see. And rats are grey. Henry's golden brown.' He examined Henry's podgy cheeks. 'And he's just gone and ruined his diet all over again!' he declared.

Mrs Ponsonby peered more closely. 'Hmm.' She sounded doubtful. 'I'm not well-up with the anatomy of rodents,' she admitted. There was a pause. 'Perhaps you are right.'

'Oh, we are. It's Henry!' Relief brought tears to Mandy's eyes. 'You were right, Mrs Ponsonby! Henry did the sensible thing and headed for cover. He must have crept into Chrissie's hamper when she left it outside on the grass. Trust Henry to head for food!'

Sure now of Henry's status as adorable pet, Mrs Ponsonby moved in to study him. 'He certainly is a charming little chap,' she agreed. 'Here, Mandy, give him to me. Let me have a good look!'

Mandy took a deep breath. She could hardly refuse, she decided. Carefully she handed Henry over. 'Hold him gently under the tummy,' she said. 'Cup your hands a little bit more . . . oh!'

'*Oh*!' Mrs Ponsonby gave a little yelp and a shiver. 'He tickles!' She opened her fingers and flattened her palms, then took her hands away with a sudden jerk.

Henry dropped on to the table, landed on all fours, and took a surprised look round. Then he scrambled down the nearest table leg.

'Watch out!' James ran to close the door. Henry scuttled across the floor. He sniffed and twitched this way and that, zigzagging across the room.

'Got him!' Mandy cried. She almost cupped her hands over the top of him, but he darted sideways and vanished under the bottom of another, narrower door.

Mandy sagged forward in dismay.

'It's OK. I think it's some sort of storeroom or cupboard!' James seized the handle and turned it. 'It's locked!'

'No, I saw it open a crack. Something must be caught on the inside!' Mandy was right behind him, adding her weight. They pulled at the door with all their might.

There was a small cry as the door gave way. Someone stepped out of the storeroom. It was Leanne. She stared at them, her face pale, her green eyes wide with fright, her red hair tumbling about her cheeks. Safe between her trembling hands she held Henry.

The full story came out, in the clubroom at Riverside. The search parties gathered happily, compared notes and congratulated one another. Apologies flew from villager to visitor. News went round that everyone was safe.

'And we're ready for the barbecue!' Mrs Ponsonby announced. She took full credit for assisting in Henry and Leanne's rescue. 'It was nothing!' she murmured. 'Really, nothing at all!'

Mandy grinned at James. 'It's mostly Blackie we should thank!' she whispered. 'Without him, we'd never have got on to Justin's track in the first place!'

James had delivered Henry and Blackie safely back home. While his dad fitted a new lock to the cage, James had weighed him. He was definitely a few grammes heavier, but content. The hamster was now fast asleep after his long adventure.

Mrs Ponsonby revelled in the happy ending. She reminded them once more of the barbecue, then pointed to an approaching figure. 'But wait, here comes Mr Western! Why, Sam, surely you've heard the good news?'

Sam Western stopped in the midst of the happy group. He was not a comfortable man. He cleared his throat. 'That's a matter of opinion,' he mumbled.

'Oh, come now, we've admitted our mistake. Mr Parker Smythe has telephoned the leader of the council to give his support to the caravan site. Let bygones be bygones, eh?'

Mandy saw Mr Western swallow hard. 'That's as maybe. But I thought it only right to come and tell you another bit of "good" news.' He surveyed his eager audience. 'I've just been speaking to my farm manager, Dennis Saville, and it seems one of my lads has been to him with a confession. He tells Dennis he took a Land-rover for a spin earlier this week, without asking permission. He brought it across country, down to the river . . .' There was a pause.

'Speak up, Sam Western!' Ernie Bell's voice growled from the back of the crowd. Half the village had congregated in the field.

'Well, the lad's a novice behind the wheel. And, to cut a long story short, he knocked into a couple of trees by the tennis courts. That's it!' He finished abruptly, overcome with embarrassment.

There was another pause. Then someone cheered. Soon everyone was smiling and shouting and shaking hands.

'And I'll tell you something else.' Ernie sidled up to Mandy. 'Walter's got his geraniums back.'

She thought he meant there'd been a miracle. 'That's fantastic!'

'Not the *same* geraniums, you understand.' Ernie tutted. 'Steady on. No, Walter's got new pots and new geraniums. Pretty as a picture, they look, standing on his front wall!'

'Where from?'

'From Mrs Platt. She thought it was only neighbourly, so she drove over to Walton earlier this afternoon and bought some fine new plants. She says the twins must pay for them out of their pocket money.'

Mandy nodded thoughtfully. 'You know, Vicki was really sorry in the end. And I think Justin was too, deep down.' She looked round, but they'd gone from the field.

'Aye well, they'll feel it in their pockets, and that's no bad thing, I say.' Ernie ambled off, saying that he might come back for the barbecue. 'Just to see what it's like, mind,' he growled. 'I'm not one for new-fangled ideas like open-air cooking, but I might just stick my nose in and take a look!'

The glowing faces round the barbecue that evening were proof of how well things had turned out.

The clouds had cleared away, a full moon shone down.

Imogen came along with her mum and dad, James was there with Blackie. Brandon came early with his little brother and sister. The McFarlanes brought a free jar of toffees, the Hardys came from the pub with soft drinks. Bert Burnley, the farmer, had good news from the council leader. 'The caravans stay here at Riverside for the rest of the summer!' he announced. Adam Hope hugged Emily and led the chorus of cheers.

Mandy stood between her mum and dad, her face aching with so much smiling. Gran and Grandad were there to join the celebrations. The whole village was united again. And there was Mrs Ponsonby, the 'heroine' of the day, describing for the umpteenth time the part she had played in the rescue of Leanne and Henry.

'The poor girl had no one to turn to,' she explained to Walter Pickard. 'So she just hid away in the clubhouse, too miserable to come out. Apparently, she was absolutely convinced that she would get the blame for the hamster's disappearance! And then when I went in there to make sandwiches, she squeezed herself into that tiny store cupboard, poor child, still hoping to avoid discovery!'

Mandy listened. 'Just a second,' she grinned at her parents. 'I've had an idea!'

Adam Hope took a deep breath. 'Be warned!' he told the others.

Mandy sped across the grass to Mrs Ponsonby's side. 'There's only one thing I still feel sorry about,' she dropped in casually. She stared up at the starlit sky.

'Oh, what's that?' Mrs Ponsonby couldn't see any dents in the perfect conclusion.

'It's poor Leanne. She has to go home tomorrow, back to Birmingham. She can't keep pets where she lives. But she loves animals, she really does!'

'Hmm.' Mrs Ponsonby looked thoughtful.

Mandy rushed on. 'Of course, their school could keep a pet, couldn't it? I mean, Kingsmill would be able to have a hamster in their biology lab, just like Walton.' She sighed. 'I expect that's the closest Leanne could get to having her own pet. Only I don't think Kingsmill has one at present . . .' She allowed her voice to tail off.

'Hmm.' By now, Mrs Ponsonby's thoughts were racing ahead. 'Would you excuse me, Mandy my dear. Now, where's that nice child with the blonde hair? Sonia, isn't it? Ah, Sonia, there you are! Just a minute, my dear, may I have a word with you?' And she trotted off.

Mandy grinned. Her stomach bubbled with excitement. It was her last wish for the evening; her parting gift for Leanne.

The Kingsmill School mini-bus stood at the gate, ready to depart. It was eleven o'clock on Saturday morning. The roof rack was piled high with rucksacks, all covered and tied down under a tarpaulin. The kids were piling on to the bus, while Mandy stood with James, who carried Henry inside his cage for a last farewell.

'Bye!' Mandy shouted. Ben gave her a thumbs-up sign as he parked himself on the back seat. Marcie waved both hands and grinned. Sonia climbed on next. She grinned over her shoulder at Mandy. 'I suppose the countryside wasn't so bad after all!' she laughed. Then Paul climbed on, with his football tucked safely under one arm. And, just as Leanne came to say goodbye to Mandy, James and Henry, Mrs Ponsonby drove her car into the field.

Mandy held her breath. Mrs Ponsonby got out and opened the back of her car. She took a large, square object from the boot. It was covered in a piece of light, white fabric. Grandly she carried it towards Leanne.

'Now, before you say anything about this, I've

checked with your headmistress on the telephone, and she's perfectly willing for the school to take Elizabeth. And she promised to phone your mother, and your mother has agreed. So, no worry on that score!' She held out the box for Leanne to take.

'Elizabeth?' Leanne frowned. She glanced at Mandy.

Mandy looked back, all wide-eyed innocence.

'Elizabeth the First,' Mrs Ponsonby explained. 'Daughter of Henry the Eighth, you know. Most appropriate. With a smile and a final grand gesture, she whisked away the cloth.

A pretty cream hamster with dark brown eyes nestled in the straw on the bottom of a wooden cage. Her eyes were huge and round, her ears neat and tufted. A band of white under her chin and round her neck shone clean and bright. She twitched her whiskers and blinked, then came forward to the front of her cage to say hello.

'Elizabeth the First,' Leanne repeated under her breath. She was mesmerised.

'I went over to Walton first thing this morning,' Mrs Ponsonby went on. 'The man in the pet shop says she's a good natured little creature, ideal for being with children.' She paused and glanced towards the mini-bus. 'There's only one teenie-

weenie little problem.' Everyone craned out of the window to take a look at the new Kingsmill hamster. 'Who will take care of Elizabeth for the rest of the summer?'

Mandy thought she saw Mrs Ponsonby wink. Leanne was too busy gazing at the hamster to notice.

'Leanne!' they shouted, without a shadow of a doubt.

'Leanne should keep her!'

'She knows all about hamsters!'

'She's the expert!'

Leanne blushed and smiled, and tears of happiness filled her eyes. 'Thank you,' she whispered to Mrs Ponsonby.

Mrs Ponsonby put one arm round her shoulder and squeezed it. 'You should thank Mandy and James,' she said gently.

'Thank you,' Leanne managed to say. 'For everything.' She carried the cage on to the bus, and was surrounded by friends who all wanted a good view of the new school hamster.

'Thank you.' Chrissie leaned out of the driver's seat and smiled at Mrs Ponsonby. 'That was very kind. And we'll be back on Monday with a new gang. See you then?'

As the bus drove off, Mandy noticed Mrs Ponsonby

take a lace hankie from her handbag. She gave a genteel sniff and dabbed her eyes.

'Say goodbye, Henry!' Mandy said. She waved them out of sight.

But Henry, back on his diet of lettuce leaves and dried oats, was hard at work on his exercise wheel. It rattled steadily as James and Mandy carried him down to the river, kicked off their shoes and stuck their feet in the cool, clear water. Mandy lifted Henry out of his cage and sat him on her lap in the full sunlight. He fidgeted, then curled up to sleep. She stroked him softly and began to daydream. The bright river flowed by, Henry snored. She was completely happy.

Hamster
in the
Holly

One

'Twelve more days till Christmas!' Mandy
Hope and her mother staggered into the
kitchen at Animal Ark, loaded down with heavy
carrier bags. Big snowflakes that had settled
lightly on Mandy's fair hair began to melt in
the warmth.

'Make way!' Adam Hope jumped up from his
seat at the table. He cleared a space for the bags.
'What did you buy, the whole shop?'

Mandy dumped the carrier bags. 'Christmas
crackers, candles, cards, wrapping-paper, tinsel,
some new Christmas tree lights, some more

silver baubles, a new star for the top of the tree—'

'Whoa!' Her dad begged her to stop and went to help Emily Hope with the rest of the shopping. 'I was joking when I said the whole of the shop!'

Mandy and her mum had driven into Walton after Saturday morning surgery. It was the last-but-one weekend before Christmas, and the small Yorkshire town where Mandy went to school had been chock-a-block with people frantically buying presents.

'Never again!' Emily Hope sighed, taking off her thick jacket and shaking off the snow. 'I don't want to see another Father Christmas's grotto or hear "Away in a Manger" ever again!'

'Hot chocolate!' Mandy's dad announced. 'That's the remedy for tired shoppers.'

Emily ran a hand through her long red hair, then looked at her watch. 'Is there time? Afternoon surgery begins in fifteen minutes, and I want to pop into the residential unit to take a look at the Border collie with the broken ribs before that.'

'Done it.' Adam Hope brought milk to the boil, then poured it into mugs and stirred in the chocolate powder. 'And I've checked the duck with the cut foot, the cat with the eye infection, and the bull-terrier with the gashed face.'

'Oh, thanks!' Mrs Hope smiled and took a steaming mug. 'Leave those bags for now, Mandy. Come and put your feet up for five minutes.'

'I can't.' Mandy pulled out the Christmas tree star. 'James is coming to rehearse our parts.'

James Hunter, Mandy's best friend, had arranged to come to Animal Ark to work with her on *The Little Mermaid*, Walton School's Christmas play.

'I thought wild horses wouldn't drag you and James on to a stage,' Adam Hope teased. 'Isn't that what you've said before now?'

'Please don't remind me!' Mandy took her mug to the window and saw James step out of his father's car, which had just pulled up.

'Don't you usually leave the prancing about, as you call it, to the likes of Susan Collins?'

'*Da-ad*!' Mandy pleaded. The thought of performing on stage in next week's end-of-term show filled her with dread. 'Mrs Winterton *made* me.'

'Count yourself lucky you don't have to wear

a mermaid's tail.' Emily Hope smiled.

'Yes, but I have to *sing*!' Mandy wailed. She flounced out of the kitchen to open the door to James. 'I have loads of complicated lines to speak. And worst of all, Mrs Winterton says I have to learn how to cackle!'

'That's not a cackle, that's a croak,' James pointed out in a bored voice. 'Witches have this special laugh that's kind of thin and wicked. Try again.'

Mandy sagged and sighed. Then she took a deep breath. '*Hah-hah! Ah-hah-hah!*'

'That's a moan.'

'*Aah-ha-ha-hah!*' She tried again, angrily this time.

'A shout,' James said dismissively. He took off his glasses and wiped them on the sleeve of his fleece jacket.

'*Haagh-aah-haaaagh!*'

Adam Hope poked his head round the kitchen door. 'Can you make less noise, Mandy, love? You're frightening the animals.'

Afternoon surgery was now well underway.

Mandy glowered across the room. 'Blame James. He keeps on making me do my cackle.'

Adam Hope couldn't hide a smile. 'Is that what it was?'

'Yes. I'm the wicked Witch of the Sea who makes a spell to change the Little Mermaid's fish-tail into a pair of legs so she can dance for the human prince she's fallen in love with . . .' Mandy launched into a description of the action.

'Spare me the details, love,' her dad cut in. 'Your mum and I will be seeing it next week anyway, so don't spoil it. Must dash. See you later.'

Mandy kept on glowering. 'The wicked witch!' she muttered in disgust. 'I have to wear a floaty black costumey-thing, and a pointy hat.'

'A pointy nose and chin?' James chipped in.

'Ha-ha!' She looked in the window at her reflection and pulled a witch-face. 'Very funny. Anyway, what about you?' James was one of the prince's courtiers, a minor part that demanded both singing and dancing. 'You have to wear a white silk shirt and make-up.'

'Don't remind me!' he shuddered. 'How did we let ourselves get roped into this?'

Mandy shook her head. 'We were in the wrong place at the wrong time.' Their music teacher, Mrs Winterton, had swooped on them in the biology lab one day after school. They'd stayed behind to clean out Henry the Eighth's cage and she'd spotted them at the very moment when she was desperate to cast the witch in the play.

'Mandy Hope!' Mrs Winterton had cried. 'You're a confident, outgoing sort of girl, just right for the part.' Then she'd turned to James. 'And James Hunter, you're perfect for Fourth Courtier. Not a big role, but you'll look splendid in the scene where the Mermaid dances for the Prince!'

'You can't say no to Mrs Winterton,' James agreed. 'She doesn't give you a chance.'

Before they knew it, they'd put Henry the hamster back into his cage and joined the first rehearsal. That had been six weeks ago. The real performance was next week, and the music teacher was *still* sighing over Mandy's cackle.

'Go home this weekend and rehearse a really wicked laugh,' she'd told Mandy, then she'd turned to James in near-despair. 'Mandy's witch isn't evil enough. Lock her in a room and make her practise. Don't come back to school on Monday unless she's got it absolutely right!'

'Do it again!' James ordered. They'd been working for nearly an hour.

'*Waagh-haagh-haagh-ha-ha-ha-haagh!*' Mandy screeched.

'Got it!' James gasped, fixing his glasses firmly on his nose and staring at her. 'Mandy, that was the most amazing cackle I ever heard!'

Rehearsal over, Mandy and James decided to help out at Animal Ark by clearing the snow that had started to settle in the carpark. They hurried across the yard with shovels, through the whirling flakes which blotted out the surrounding hills sloping down towards Welford village.

'Uh-oh!' James spotted the round figure of Mrs Ponsonby as she lifted Pandora, her Pekinese dog, from the car. Her lively mongrel, Toby, scampered down by himself and rolled in the snow, his jaws snapping excitedly at it.

'Mandy, dear! And James! Could you please help me?' The fussy old lady struggled to tuck Pandora under one arm and put up her umbrella at the same time.

Mandy ran to hold the umbrella over Pandora, who was wearing a tartan coat over

her long cream fur. The dog snuffled and leaned out towards the floating flakes of snow.

'I don't have an appointment,' Mrs Ponsonby explained as she struggled towards the surgery, 'but I'm worried about Pandora, so I thought it best to bring her in.'

'What's wrong with her?' Mandy stumbled alongside, watching James playing with Toby in the snow.

The old lady shook her head and sighed tragically. 'Poor little Pandora is so delicate, and she hates the cold. One can never be too sure.'

'But what happened, exactly?' Holding open the surgery door, Mandy glimpsed Jean Knox, the receptionist, filling in forms at the desk. And through the open door of one of the treatment rooms, she could see her mum checking the stitches of Bill, a bull-terrier who'd been in a fight.

Mrs Ponsonby tossed back her head and stepped inside with the supposedly sick Pekinese. 'Pandora *sneezed*! Twice!' she told Jean. 'We need to see a vet immediately!'

Two more patients crossed paths with Mrs Ponsonby on their way out of Animal Ark. 'Oh dear, look at the weather!' said Marjorie Spry to her identical twin sister, Joan.

Or was it the other way around? Mandy could never tell the difference between the two old ladies from The Riddings. The second twin was carrying their young black-and-white cat, Patch, in a small wire cage.

'However shall we drive home in all this snow?' Joan or Marjorie fussed at the doorstep.

'Why not leave your car here and let me drive you home, ladies?' David Gill, a farmer from Greystones, was also on his way out. He was tall and steady, and took all weathers in his long stride. 'I have my Land-rover parked outside if you don't mind putting up with a young pig I've got in the back.'

As Mrs Ponsonby sailed forward demanding attention and the two nervous spinsters dithered in the doorway, Mandy grinned at James, who was having a snowball fight with Toby in the yard. The dog dodged and barked delightedly.

'A pig?' one of the Miss Sprys fluttered. 'Oh dear! Oh my!'

'He won't hurt you,' Mr Gill assured her. 'And I'll send a farmhand along to fetch your car when the snow dies down. He'll drive it along to The Riddings for you two ladies, no problem!'

So the twins accepted, and took Patch home in the Land-rover. Meanwhile, Jean explained to Mrs Ponsonby that Pandora's condition wasn't life-threatening and that she must wait in the queue.

'Queue?' Mrs Ponsonby looked round archly, as if she didn't recognise the word.

There was a row of owners sitting quietly with their hamsters, rabbits, cats and dogs.

'But Pandora *sneezed*!' she repeated, cuddling the dog close to her ample bosom. 'It could be pneumonia!'

Jean read down her list for the next appointment. 'Joanna Davey and Mabel, Treatment Room One, please!'

Mandy spied a small white furry creature in a cage. She didn't recognise its owner – a young, brown-haired woman in a bright orange fleece and black ski-pants. As they headed off for a consultation with Adam Hope, Mandy slipped past Mrs Ponsonby and round the reception desk into the small, scrubbed treatment room. 'Can I help?' she whispered to her dad.

Mr Hope nodded. 'Who have we here?' he

asked the newcomer to Welford.

'Mabel. She's a Chinese hamster, expecting babies in about a week.' Joanna Davey lifted her pet out of the cage and put her gently on the table. 'I noticed she was a bit under the weather when I fed her this morning, and since she's pregnant, I thought I'd better bring her in.'

Mandy crouched so that she was at eye-level with the table. 'Mabel on the table.' She smiled to herself. The chubby hamster was pure white, with ruby-red eyes. She squatted on her haunches and clasped her tiny pink forefeet together, close to her nose. Her white whiskers twitched, and her little round ears flicked this way and that.

Adam Hope examined Mabel from the opposite side of the table, taking her temperature, then looking at her nose, mouth and eyes. 'Yes, she has a runny nose,' he observed. 'She's probably caught a chill in this cold weather.'

'Nothing serious?' Joanna asked, gently stroking Mabel with her forefinger. The hamster nuzzled against it, then hopped into her cupped hand.

'Probably not. The remedy is to rig up an infra-red light at the side of her cage. Turn on the heat and switch her diet to seed and water, nothing else. If she's not better in a couple of days, give us a ring.' Mr Hope smiled at the little white creature as she tried, fell back, then succeeded in scrambling up Joanna's arm and on to her shoulder.

Joanna picked her up with the other hand and put her back in the cage. She'd taken in the brisk, plain instructions. 'Anything else?'

'Oh yes. Do you have other hamsters?'

Joanna Davey nodded. 'Two. Honey and Marmalade. A cream-coloured satin-coat and a cinnamon angora.'

'Well, in that case, keep Mabel isolated from them. You don't want them all sick at the same time.' Adam Hope peeled off his surgical gloves and asked Mandy to wipe down the table with a disinfected cloth. 'Remember, if you're at all worried, give us a ring.'

'Thanks. We're new to Welford, so this is our first visit to Animal Ark.' The young woman stood at the door, carrying the hamster cage between both hands. 'You've been really helpful. I hope I haven't made too much fuss.'

Mandy saw her dad smile, then wince as he overheard Mrs Ponsonby's loud voice in the waiting-room. 'Not at all,' he assured Joanna Davey. 'In fact, you've probably made Mandy's day. She loves hamsters!'

Mandy grinned and blushed. 'I'd like to see Honey and Marmalade too,' she confessed.

The young woman grinned back. 'Any time. We've moved into a house on the main street in the village, next to the post office.'

'Great! Thank you!' Mandy was delighted: two more hamsters for her to get to know! She loved the small, furry, friendly creatures with their fat cheek pouches and squat, square bodies.

'Well, how about tomorrow afternoon?' Joanna suggested.

Mandy's eyes lit up, then faded. 'I'm sorry, I can't.' Rehearsal at school, Sunday afternoon. More cackling.

'She has an appointment with a mermaid,' Adam Hope added jokingly.

'Well, any time,' Joanna said sweetly, turning to go and almost bumping into Mrs Ponsonby. 'Come and see Mabel's babies when they're born. Remember, the house next to the post office – the one with the bright green door.'

She made her way across the busy waiting-room, then paused. 'We'll see you soon,' she called to Mandy. 'Thanks, and bye!'

Two

Sunday dawned cold and crisp.

'The holly and the ivy . . .' Adam Hope
crooned, lazing over the weekend papers.
'When they are both full-grown . . . *buh-buh-bu-
bu-buh* that are in the wood . . .' He blew the
tune through puffed-out cheeks.

Mandy giggled. 'You look like a hamster!'

'You and hamsters!' he teased. 'By the way,
Joanna Davey rang early this morning to say the
infra-red treatment was doing the trick for
Mabel. That was nice of her, wasn't it?'

'Yes, I liked her.' Mandy was picking up scraps

of paper from the windowsill, chairs and next to the toaster. The paper had lines from the school play written down for her to learn while she went about her business. There were bits stuck to the mirror in her bedroom, next to the pony posters on the wall, others on Jean's desk in Reception, and one on the back of the bathroom door. 'I'll never learn these in time for next Monday,' she sighed.

'You will.' Emily Hope appeared at the door, bringing the cold wind in with her. She stamped the snow from her boots and took off her coat. 'I've just brought in a badger that's been hit by a car,' she reported. 'Joanna Davey's husband, John, spotted him and flagged me down. I was just on my way back from dropping off that stray hedgehog at Rosa's Refuge.'

'A badger!' Mandy gasped. 'How is it?'

'Well, he was unconscious at first,' her mother replied, 'but he came round as I drove him back here. Probably concussed from the accident, but I don't think he's broken any bones. I've put him in the unit for observation.'

Keen to go and take a look at the badger, Mandy offered to clean the cats' cages in the residential unit while she was there. As she made her way through to the unit her mum reminded her that there was only an hour to go before James's dad arrived to drive her and James over to Walton for their rehearsal.

'And you have to have lunch first!' Emily called.

But to Mandy the injured badger was much more interesting than lunch. The wild creature lay quietly in a cage usually used for large dogs, his stumpy legs stretched straight out, his coarse grey fur still damp from the melted snow. He heard Mandy approach and raised his head without stirring the rest of his bruised body.

'Poor you!' Mandy put her face close to the cage and gazed in. The badger's flat, black-and-white striped head sank back on to the blanket. 'But we'll look after you now. You'll soon be better, then we'll take you back to where we found you and you'll be able to make your way back to your nice warm den.'

'Sett,' Emily Hope corrected quietly. She'd followed Mandy through the back of the cottage into the unit, and stood behind her to observe the concussed animal. 'Badgers live in setts.'

Mandy sighed. 'I know. Isn't he gorgeous?'

'Yes. There's something special about

badgers,' her mother agreed, smiling. 'Maybe it's because they're nocturnal, so we hardly ever see them.'

'More than that.' Mandy backed away to give the patient chance to rest. 'They're strong, and . . .' She sought for the right word and found it. '. . . secret.'

'And quite fierce when necessary,' Emily Hope added, staying to help Mandy with the cleaning. For a while they talked about badgers' habits in the wild. 'I felt when I rescued him from the roadside and brought him back here that it was a kind of privilege to be allowed to help such a magnificent creature,' she concluded.

Mandy smiled at her mum. 'I think that about every animal who comes to Animal Ark,' she confessed.

'I know you do,' Mrs Hope smiled back. 'That's why you're going to be a great vet when you grow up, Mandy Hope!'

'A better vet than actress,' Mandy said glumly a few hours later. 'I'll never be able to learn those lines in time.' She'd struggled through the first act of the play and retreated to the biology lab

to sit with Henry the hamster. Mrs Winterton
was still in the assembly hall, putting some of
the dancers, including James, through their
paces.

Henry ignored her gloomy predictions. He
and Mandy were good friends. She and James
had looked after him during one long summer
holiday, when they'd put him on a fruit and
vegetable diet to help the chubby little brown-
and-white creature to lose weight. Henry hadn't
appreciated their efforts, and had promptly
escaped into a picnic hamper, where he'd
munched his way through a pile of sandwiches
and cake.

In fact, the school hamster was good at
escaping, though you wouldn't believe it to look
at him now. Mandy gazed into the cage on the
biology lab shelf as Henry trundled away inside
his exercise wheel. His short legs worked
furiously, his short-sighted eyes fixed firmly
ahead as he dedicated himself to keeping fit.

' "I already know what you want!" ' Mandy
recited her first lines as the Witch of the Sea as
she gazed at her favourite hamster. The Witch
was talking to the Little Mermaid, alias Susan
Collins. (*Cackle, cackle.*) ' "You want to get rid of

your fish-tail and have two stumps to walk on like human beings." ' (*Cackle*) ' "It is very stupid of you!" '

'Er, Mandy . . .' James cut into her fourth cackle. He was standing at the door of the lab with small, fair-haired Daniel Winterton, the music teacher's seven-year-old son. 'I told Daniel he could come and look at Henry.'

Mandy went on with her lines. ' "You've come just in the nick of time! After tomorrow's sunrise, I could do nothing to help you for another year!" ' She laughed again, plucking imaginary toads from her hair and shoulders.

Daniel pulled a scared face and backed away.

'It's OK,' James coaxed. 'Take no notice of Mandy. Come and see the hamster.'

The younger boy sidled into the room after James and crept up to Henry's cage. The class pet trundled gamely on inside his wheel.

'Daniel was bored,' James explained. 'He's had to sit through weeks of rehearsal while his mum's been busy with the play. And it just so happens he likes hamsters, don't you, Daniel?'

'I love them.' His pale, round face had broken into a smile as he watched Henry turn the wheel. 'I had one when I was four years old. I called him Norvik. He liked to climb up the curtains. He was a satin-coated Himalayan hamster with red eyes.' The smile faded as he spoke.

'What happened to him?' Mandy asked.

'He died.' Daniel sighed. 'We found him under a pile of wood shavings in the corner of his cage. He probably felt poorly while we were at school and crept in there. When we got home, he was dead.'

'I'm sorry,' Mandy said quietly, gazing over Daniel's shoulder at sturdy, lively Henry and feeling glad that he was healthy. She knew that small pets like hamsters could go downhill very quickly once they grew ill. 'Maybe you can get another hamster soon.'

Quickly Daniel Winterton shook his head. 'Mum doesn't like hamsters or mice, and because Dad isn't around much to help any more, she says I'll have to wait until I'm older and able to look after it myself. Anyway, it wouldn't be the same. Norvik was special.'

As his voice trailed off, Henry stopped trundling and hopped out of his wheel. He came to the front of his cage in short, nervous bursts, then poked his little pink nose through the bars.

'He's saying hello.' Mandy felt sorry for the sad little boy. She'd noticed him in the assembly hall where they rehearsed the Christmas play, hidden away in a corner, reading or writing in a notebook he always carried with him. He looked lonely, but Mrs Winterton seemed too busy to notice.

'Hello,' Daniel whispered to Henry, reaching out gently to touch the hamster's nose.

Henry sniffed and sat up on his back legs, front paws dangling, as if begging for food.

'You've had your tea!' Mandy scolded with a smile. She turned to Daniel. 'What do you write in your notebook?'

'Stories.' He blushed to the roots of his fair hair. 'About hamsters. Would you like to see?'

Mandy blinked back her surprise and nodded.

So Daniel brought out his notebook, and offered it to Mandy. She took it and opened it at the first page. '*The Adventures of Norvik*', she read, 'by Daniel Winterton. Part One: The Castle on the Hill.'

'It's about a hamster who fights to save his family from foxes who live in the castle,' Daniel

said earnestly, his grey eyes wide and shining. 'Norvik is the hero.'

Mandy flicked over the pages and read out loud: ' "Come back!" the Fox King shouted at his band of cowardly foxes. "Stay and fight!" He pulled a big, sharp sword from his belt and pointed it at Norvik. "Prepare to meet your death!" '

'Wow!' James raised his eyebrows. 'That's pretty exciting. What happens to Norvik next?'

'He wins the fight,' Daniel explained. 'Then he rescues his brothers and sisters, then he sets fire to the Fox King's castle and all the hamsters escape.'

'Wow!' It was Mandy's turn to be impressed. She loved the look of the little book, with its closely printed words and colourful, hand-drawn pictures.

'Daniel! There you are!' Mrs Winterton bustled into the lab. She was obviously taking a well-earned break from rehearsals and had come looking for her son. She was a thin, pretty woman with thick, jet-black hair and big brown eyes, not at all like Daniel. Today she was dressed for action in a long, pale blue shirt and black leggings.

'I might have known this was where you'd be!' she exclaimed, noticing Henry in his cage. 'Hamsters!' She raised her finely arched eyebrows at Mandy and James. 'I can't keep him away.'

'Look, Mum, he's saying hello.' Daniel pointed to Henry, who was still grabbing the cage wire with his front paws and poking his nose through the gaps.

'Come on, Daniel, I haven't time to look. I've a million things to do,' Mrs Winterton said. 'I want you back in the hall where I can keep an eye on you. And Mandy and James, could you go to the art room for costume fittings with Miss Temple? You have five minutes before we start on Act Two, so please get a move on.'

'Bye, Henry!' Daniel gave the hamster one last stroke.

'You can see him again soon,' his mother promised, waiting impatiently by the door. She marched her son down the corridor to the hall.

'Be good, Henry,' James joked, tickling his stomach through the wire mesh.

The hamster seemed to sigh as he dropped to the floor of his cage and waddled away. Back to the exercise wheel: *squeak-squeak-squeak.*

Mandy took a long, last look, smiled, then turned off the light.

'That's good, Mandy!' Mrs Winterton was happy with her cackle at last.

It was the scene where the mermaid's sisters visited the witch to plead for her life. The Witch of the Sea drove a hard bargain, telling the sisters that the Little Mermaid must kill her beloved prince in order to save herself. The mermaid sisters did a dance to sad music and sang words which Mrs Winterton had written herself.

Mandy held up her hands and wiggled her fingers in a scary, witchlike way. She drove the mermaids away with a fierce shriek.

'Very good!' From her seat at the piano, the music teacher praised Mandy's dramatic exit. 'Mermaids, you must hold the long notes. And more volume, please. Now, one more time!'

Her part finished for now, Mandy slipped from the stage and made her way across the hall. She was looking for Daniel, to ask him more about *The Adventures of Norvik.*

'Have you seen Daniel Winterton?' she asked Susan Collins.

The star of the show was busy learning her lines at the back of the hall. 'Not lately,' she murmured, without looking up.

'Try the art room,' Vicky Simpson suggested. Vicky was packing away the violin that she played in the school orchestra and taking it along the corridor to the music department's store room. 'Miss Temple's still in there doing costumes. Maybe Daniel got bored and went along.'

'No, sorry, I haven't seen him.' Miss Temple said when Mandy went to ask. James was standing very still while the biology teacher stuck dressmakers' pins into his shirt. It was too big and needed to be taken in.

'Try the biology lab,' he suggested. 'You know . . . hamster . . . Daniel . . . *Ouch!*' One of the pins pricked his arm.

'Don't move!' Miss Temple ordered.

So Mandy backtracked down the corridor to the lab. The light was off, the room in darkness. Not here either, she said to herself. But something made her step inside the door.

It's too quiet! She listened for the squeak of

Henry's wheel and heard only silence. *Perhaps he's asleep. No, hamsters come out at night. He should be moving about.* Worried thoughts flashed through her head as she crept across the darkened room, past the long benches where the classes did their practical biology work, towards the shelf where Henry's cage stood. The only light came from the street lamps in the road outside, which cast a strange orange glare.

'Henry?' Mandy leaned forward to examine the cage.

Nothing. No squeak of the wheel, no curious little brown and white face at the bars.

'Henry!' Gripped by real fear, Mandy reached out for the cage door. It swung open at her touch.

'Oh, no!' Swiftly she looked inside, amongst the piles of wood shavings, under the plastic toy log in one corner, behind the exercise wheel, inside the small nest-box where the hamster slept. Empty!

Mandy backed off, looking wildly along the shelf. She fell to the floor and scrabbled between the benches and stools. Nothing.

Then she got up and ran for the assembly

hall. She flew down the big room to the piano where the music teacher was playing. 'Please stop, Mrs Winterton!' she begged, her hair flying across her face, her arms waving in the direction from which she'd come.

'Mandy, whatever is the matter?' The teacher stood up. Everyone on stage stared at Mandy. Susan and Vicky came forward from the back of the hall. Daniel crept to his mother's side.

'Oh, quick!' she gasped. 'I need some help. Henry's escaped from his cage. We have to find him!'

Three

'Calm down!' Mrs Winterton called above the gasps and excited chatter. She got up on to the stage to issue instructions. 'Let's all break off from rehearsal for ten minutes and set up a search party to find the school hamster. Mandy, you take a group back into the biology lab. James, you choose four or five people to help you look along the ground-floor corridor. And Susan, you can cover the art room and the home economics room.'

Reluctantly Susan Collins put down her script. 'All this for a hamster!' she grumbled.

'Not just any old hamster,' James told her as he gathered his group and headed for the corridor. 'Henry's a kind of school mascot. We can't let him wander off and get into trouble.'

'He might fall off a high shelf,' Mandy muttered, 'or crawl into one of the ovens in the home economics room.' Her imagination was working full-tilt. 'Hamsters are short-sighted,' she explained.

'He might climb inside a cupboard,' James added.

'Or into someone's open locker and then get locked in!' Mandy was really panicking now. She noticed Daniel's worried face as he kept close to his mother's side. 'Come on, Daniel. You can join our group and help us look.'

Daniel frowned and shuffled towards her. 'What if Henry manages to get outside?' he whispered.

Mandy shook her head. 'Don't even say that! He'll freeze to death. You know how cold it is out there!' The idea sent her running back to the lab. 'Let's look under the cupboards,' she said to Vicky and her two friends, Claire and Michelle. 'Daniel and I will look in Miss Temple's storeroom.'

As they split up to begin a thorough search, the biology teacher came in. 'Try not to worry too much,' she told the children. 'Henry makes quite a habit of escaping, remember. And he always turns up safe and sound.'

'The Adventures of Henry!' Mandy muttered to Daniel, trying to take on board the biology teacher's more cheerful view. Together they passed the cage and paused to look behind the piles of textbooks next to it. 'The bold hamster teetered on the edge of the shelf, staring death in the eye! Panting heavily, he launched himself into midair and plummeted to the ground. Down came the pile of books, crashing after him, pages fluttering in a mysterious wind . . . !'

Daniel refused to smile. His face was shocked and pale. 'How did he get out of his cage in the first place?'

Mandy carried on to the store, opened cupboards and peered inside. They smelled of rubber tubing, and a whiff of gas from bunsen-burners stored there. But there was no Henry. 'I don't know.' Slowly she turned her head to study Daniel, who was on his hands and knees beside her. His eyes were troubled, so Mandy did her best to cheer him up. 'Come on, Henry can't have gone far,' she told him. 'He has to be round here somewhere!'

'Any luck?' James put his head around the biology lab door.

Mandy shook her head. They'd been looking for five minutes, and there was no trace of the escapee.

'Me neither.' James and his group had searched the length of the ground-floor corridor. 'He's not in the lockers, or under the radiators. And I've checked with Susan's lot. He's not gobbling ingredients in the home economics room either.'

Henry often headed for food when he made his getaways. 'Is she sure?' Mandy asked doubtfully.

'Yes, I'm sure!' Susan arrived with a toss of her long dark hair. 'We've looked in all the drawers and under the cookers. He hasn't even touched the plate of biscuits Miss Temple put out for refreshments earlier this afternoon.'

'Hmm.' This was unusual. Jammy Dodgers and chocolate wafers all laid out in the room next to the biology lab – a perfect Henry treat. And they were untouched. Henry's sensitive nose must be letting him down.

They were rapidly running out of places to try.

Heavy footsteps plodded down the corridor and a new face appeared at the biology lab door.

'What's going on?' a deep voice asked. It belonged to Mr Browning, the school caretaker, who kept a careful eye on the site, even at weekends. He was short, stocky and serious, dressed for the weather in a padded jacket, with big woollen socks pulled up over his trousers, and sturdy walking-boots.

'It's the hamster,' Mrs Winterton explained, drifting by with a frazzled expression on her face as she headed for the music department storeroom, music scores and a clarinet tucked under her arm. She disappeared inside and could be heard shifting heavy instruments round the small space.

'It's not escaped again, has it?' Mr Browning tutted and frowned at Mandy as if it must be her fault.

'I'm afraid so.' Miss Temple emerged from the art room and stepped in smartly to keep the peace. 'But don't worry, Mr Browning. Henry will turn up.'

'Hmph!' The caretaker pressed his thin lips together. 'Well, he'd better put in an appearance pretty fast,' he warned. 'I'm not keeping the school open after four o'clock. That's all I'm getting paid for. Anyhow, I have my last-minute Christmas shopping to do. So in three-quarters of an hour I turf you all out and lock up for the night.'

Grumpily he swung his large bunch of keys at them, turned and stomped off down the corridor.

'Thanks for nothing!' James murmured under his breath.

Just then, Mrs Winterton reappeared. 'Er . . . Mandy, James!' she whispered, edging backwards into the corridor.

'Is it Henry?' James sprang forward.

'In here!' The music teacher held her finger to her lips to warn them to be quiet. 'At least, I think so!'

Mandy ran to follow James. 'Come on, Daniel!' The three of them crowded round Mrs Winterton.

'Look on top of the drum kit,' the teacher whispered

Sure enough, they could hear sharp little feet

scrabbling over the taut surface of the bass drum. *Rat-a-tat-tat! Swish-thump!* Henry skidded against the rim of the drum. He peered over the edge with a bewildered expression on his furry face.

'Thank heavens!' Mandy breathed a sigh of relief and edged into the cramped, airless room. 'Fetch his cage, Daniel.'

As the little boy ran to do as he was asked, his mother conferred with Mandy and James. 'I'm not too keen on being in the same room with anything like a hamster,' she confessed. She seemed out of breath and jittery. 'Mice, guinea-pigs, rats – they all make me feel uneasy. I used to leave the animal care to my husband when Daniel had his pet hamster. Is it all right if I leave you two to persuade Henry back into his cage while I take the other members of the cast to the hall and carry on with our rehearsal?'

'Of course.' James was so relieved to see Henry, he wouldn't take eyes off him as the hamster poised on the edge of the bass drum, ready to launch himself on to a nearby cymbal.

'Good,' said Mrs Winterton, relaxing slightly. 'Come along as soon as you can. We have to go through the finale before we leave – and you know what Mr Browning's like; he'll want us out on the dot!' She beat a hasty retreat.

Crash! Henry landed on the metal disc and clung on. Slowly he slipped towards the edge.

'Uh-oh!' Mandy dived across the room to catch him, tripped over a cello case and missed.

Henry dropped from the cymbal on to a keyboard and scuttled along the polished white keys.

'Henry was on a narrow ledge,' James laughed and told the hero's story. 'Below him, a grisly, giant face cried out in pain. He knew that he had only seconds to escape from the monster's horrid grasp!'

'Ha-ha!' Mandy rubbed her bruised elbows and got up. By now, Daniel had arrived with the hamster cage. James shut the door behind him. At least now there was no way out for Henry. Meanwhile, the runaway pet had jumped off the keyboard and scuttled along the table, behind a shiny French horn.

'He's vanished!' Daniel cried.

Mandy was nearest, so she clambered across guitar cases to look behind the horn. 'Gone!' she reported.

'He can't have!' James climbed over two double basses and a loudspeaker to join her.

'He has; he's vanished!' Mandy tried to think straight. She began to scour the area, looking behind clarinets and trumpets and inside empty instrument cases to see if Henry had sneaked in anywhere.

'There are so many places he could hide!' James complained.

'And we thought we were so near to cornering him!'

'We still are,' Mandy insisted. The door was closed. There were no windows for Henry to climb through. 'If we split up and take one section of the room each, we're bound to find him.'

So Daniel put the empty cage near the door and joined in. For fifteen minutes they carefully lifted and moved every single instrument in the storeroom.

'Nothing!' James sighed.

Mandy stood up and eased her stiff back. Some of the bigger instruments like the cellos and double basses were heavy.

Just then, there was a knock at the door. 'Mandy! James! Mrs Winterton says you have to come and rehearse the finale!' It was Susan's voice.

'Tell her we haven't found Henry yet,' Mandy pleaded. Her face was red and shiny from the effort of shifting the instruments.

'She says to leave Daniel to carry on looking while you two do your bit on stage. You can come back in five minutes!'

Mandy sighed.

'OK. Daniel, you heard: we'll be five minutes!'

Reluctantly they opened the door a crack, squeezed through, then shot off to the hall. They went on-stage and walked through their parts in the final song, hardly noticing what they were doing.

'Courtiers, come forward to take your bow!' Mrs Winterton ordered.

James and three other boys did as they were asked. Then James slid away, back to the storeroom.

'Witch of the Sea, come forward!' Mrs Winterton played the witch's theme music.

Mandy bowed and escaped after James.

'Daniel, are you there?' James had run down the corridor and was knocking at the door when Mandy joined him.

'Yes.' A muffled voice answered.

'Have you found Henry?'

There was a long pause, then, 'No!'

Mandy and James groaned.

'OK, let us in again, quick!' James had spotted the caretaker striding down the corridor, looking at his watch.

'We've got to get Henry back before he locks up,' Mandy hissed, hearing the jangle of keys. 'If we leave him loose, anything could happen before school opens again tomorrow morning!' The situation was getting serious, despite what Miss Temple had said earlier.

'Don't tell me!' James leaned against the door, waiting for Daniel to open it the fraction they needed to get back inside the store.

'I want to come out!' The small boy's face appeared at the crack. 'I don't like it in here by myself!'

'Right!' James was just about to slip in instead, when Mr Browning collared him and Mandy.

'Is that hamster still on the run?' the caretaker demanded, keys jingling in his pocket. 'You know it's five minutes to four.'

'We just need a bit more time,' Mandy begged.

He shook his head. 'Sorry. No can do.' He

walked on, checking rooms to right and left.

'We've got four minutes,' Mandy sighed.

'Let me out!' Daniel said again.

'OK, we're ready,' James told him. 'Are you sure Henry's nowhere near the door?'

'I told you, no! I haven't found him!' He sounded as if he was almost in tears.

So James eased open the door. Daniel came out hanging his head, carefully carrying a black violin case, and shuffled off down the corridor.

James slipped into the stuffy room to take his place, but Mandy hesitated before following him. 'Hang on, Daniel,' she called.

The little boy didn't stop, so Mandy ran after him. 'Where are you taking that violin?' she asked.

'Home,' he muttered.

'What for?' Mandy's suspicions grew. Daniel was behaving very strangely, refusing to look up or to stop.

'Mum says I have to practise.'

'I didn't know you played the violin.' She stepped in front of him. 'Anyway, when will you have time to practise before tomorrow?'

'Tonight,' he said angrily, glaring up at her. Pulling the case up in front of him, he tried to sidestep past Mandy The clumsy movement made him almost drop the case. He caught it as it slipped, but the catch clicked and the lid swung open. Inside, it was empty.

Or was it? Daniel gave a frightened cry and desperately tried to close up the case, but Mandy had seen a movement. A brown and white shape scuttled across the blue velvet interior.

'Henry!' The hamster was inside the violin case!

James heard Mandy's cry and came running, followed by Miss Temple, then Mr Browning, tramping back down the corridor to see what all the fuss was about.

Daniel Winterton froze on the spot. His brown eyes filled with tears, his bottom lip trembled. There was no room for doubt: Mandy had caught him red-handed trying to sneak Henry out of the school.

Four

'Oh, Daniel!' Mrs Winterton's face trembled with disappointment. 'How could you even think of stealing poor Henry?'

Tears spilled out of the little boy's eyes and slid down his round cheeks. 'I just really, really wanted to look after him!' he cried.

'But what would you have done with him if you'd managed to get him out of school?' Mandy asked.

They'd gathered in the biology lab: Daniel and his mother, Miss Temple, James and Mandy. Everyone else was being seen out of the building by an impatient Mr Browning. Henry was back in his cage, safe and sound.

'I would've kept him secret and put him in Norvik's old cage,' Daniel explained miserably. 'He would've been my very own pet.'

'But how?' James's logical mind ran ahead. 'Your mum would've been bound to find out. Henry's a real live animal; he needs food and water. You'd have to clean out his cage and spend loads of time talking to him so he didn't get lonely.'

'Ah!' Mrs Winterton sighed. 'I think you might have hit on something there,' she told James. 'About pets not being allowed to get lonely. I'm afraid it's Daniel who's been the lonely one lately.'

The little boy hung his head and sniffed.

'You see, his daddy's been working in London since September. He comes home for weekends and he'll be back for Christmas, but Daniel's been missing him a lot. And I've been so busy with the school show that I haven't been able to spend much time with Daniel either.'

Mandy nodded. She felt sorry for the shy, bookish boy and tried to imagine what it would be like if her own dad worked away from home.

'It's not long till Christmas,' she reminded him.

'But, Daniel, the fact remains that you shouldn't have tried to trick Mandy and James into thinking that you hadn't found Henry,' Mrs Winterton explained. 'Think how unhappy they would have been if they'd gone home believing that the school hamster was lost for good!' His mother was still disappointed in him.

'And Henry already has a nice, cosy home,' Miss Temple added, 'except for the loose door-catch here.' She took a screwdriver from a drawer and tightened the screws holding the catch in place. 'I'm fixing it so it won't work loose again,' she told Mandy and James. 'That's what must have happened before, without anyone noticing, and nifty little Henry was quick to take advantage when our backs were turned.'

'At least everything's worked out OK,' James said, hearing Mr Browning's footsteps stamping down the corridor. 'The adventures of Henry have ended happily yet again!'

'I think this lump on Tiddles' eyelid has been caused by hedgehog ticks.' Emily Hope was busy in the surgery when Mandy arrived home from school late on Monday afternoon.

After the latest nerve-wracking rehearsal for the school show, Mandy had nipped into the residential unit to reassure herself that the concussed badger was well on the road to recovery, then slipped into the treatment room to see her mum in action.

Mrs Hope was bending over Ernie Bell's cat while the old man stood to one side. Despite his frowning manner, Ernie was soft-hearted over Tiddles and his pet squirrel, Sammy.

'Is it serious?' he asked, too anxious to look round and say hello to Mandy.

'Her ears and eyelids are covered in the ticks,' she explained. 'I take it Tiddles still spends a fair amount of time outside?'

'I can't keep her in.' The elderly man shook his head. 'She's a wanderer, always out and about.'

Ernie's house was in the centre of the village, next door the Fox and Goose, where there was plenty of chance for Tiddles to mix with other cats.

'Well, she's been unlucky. The ticks are parasites, and they've decided that Tiddles is a good host now that any sensible hedgehog is hibernating for the winter.' Mrs Hope dabbed at the lump above the cat's eye with a cotton-wool swab. 'What's probably happened is that Tiddles has scratched at a tick and pulled part of it out, but left the head part embedded under her skin. Then the tiny wound has become infected and caused the eyelid to swell.'

Mandy put down her schoolbag and shuddered at the gruesome description. Tiddles had been one of the kittens she and James had found homes for after Walton, the school cat, had given birth to them in the former caretaker's kitchen.

'I'll give you some antibiotic tablets to crush up and put in Tiddles' food, and, some spray to deal with the ticks. All being well, the problem should clear up within the next few days.' Emily Hope lifted the young cat and handed him back to his owner.

The old man smiled with relief as he held his squirming pet. 'I'm thankful it's nothing worse. You hear that, Mandy?' He turned and nodded. 'Your mum's a clever lady. She knows her stuff.'

Mandy grinned back, glad that Ernie was happy. His lined, sharp-featured face had creased into deep wrinkles, so that his eyes almost disappeared beneath his bushy white eyebrows. As he and Tiddles went out, she helped her mum wipe down the treatment table.

'Good rehearsal?' Emily Hope asked, peeling off her surgical gloves. Tiddles had been her last patient of the day. She unbuttoned her white coat and led the way into Reception, where Jean Knox was finishing work.

'Awful!' Mandy groaned. 'Mrs Winterton says we have to stay behind after school every day this week, *and* go in on Saturday and Sunday afternoon!'

'It'll all be worthwhile,' her mum promised. 'Once you get up there on that stage in front of a real audience, I'm sure you'll enjoy it.'

'Ohhhh!' Mandy grimaced. 'Don't, Mum!' The thought of a real audience terrified her.

'I'll be there,' Jean promised, folding her glasses and putting them in their case. 'I've got a seat in the front row.'

'Uhhh!' Mandy sagged against the desk.

'And the whole of Welford will be there too!' Jean's eyes twinkled. 'The school show in Walton is part of our Christmas tradition. No one wants miss it.'

'We've bought our tickets already,' Emily

Hope reminded Mandy. 'So have Gran and Grandad.'

'I hope it snows and everyone gets stuck inside their houses!' Mandy exclaimed. She sank further down, longing for the bad weather to return. Since Saturday, the snow had melted, except on top of the hills. 'Then they'd have to call the whole thing off!'

Adam Hope overheard as he came out of the second treatment room. 'The holly and the ivy . . . When they are both full grown . . . *buh-buh-bu-bu-buh-bu-bu* in the wood . . .'

'I'm serious, Dad!' No one seemed to understand how bad stage fright felt. In exactly a week's time, on Monday the twenty-first of December, Mandy would have to don her witchy clothes and pointy hat to go on stage in front of hundreds of people, and cackle for real!

The week sped by and Mrs Winterton was putting on the pressure to get the show ready for Monday while Miss Temple dashed here and there with costumes and props under her arms. There wasn't even five minutes to spare for Mandy to visit Honey and Marmalade at the Daveys' new house. Then, at home, on the

Wednesday evening, Mandy's mum and dad decided that the concussed badger was fit to be returned to the wild.

'Would you like to come?' Emily Hope asked her daughter.

Mandy looked up from her homework and out of the kitchen window at a clear, starry sky. She nodded eagerly.

'Get well wrapped up, then. I'll bring the badger out to the car and meet you there.'

Mandy ran upstairs for her warmest jumper. In five minutes, she was ready and waiting in the frosty yard.

'Watch out! He's pretty impatient.' Mrs Hope lifted the cage with the badger inside into the back of the car. The sturdy creature turned swiftly in small circles, sniffing the fresh night air with his long black snout. Once in the car, he came to the front of the cage and pressed his nose against the wire mesh, his small eyes gleaming.

'Where are we going to set him free?' Mandy asked. She felt a small knot of excitement in her stomach as they set off from Animal Ark and drove carefully down the narrow lane towards the village. The headlights of the four-

wheel drive showed up every blade of stiff, frost-
covered grass and tangled bramble branches on
either side of the road.

'You know McFarlanes' post office?' Emily
Hope stopped at the junction with the main
village street to wait for two cars and a
motorbike to pass. 'There's a gap at the side of
the building, between the post office and the
row of houses where the Daveys have just moved
in.'

'I know it.' Mandy glanced over her shoulder
to check on the badger. The scared creature
had retreated to a corner of the cage, unable
to make sense of the swaying, jolting movement
of the car. He thrust his nose forward and
craned his neck towards the crack of fresh air
coming in through the open window.

'I'm guessing that gap is where he came down
when he was knocked over. There are fields at
the back of the houses, and then a small wood
– just the sort of territory where a badger would
make his sett.'

'So we'll take him down the alleyway and set
him free in the field?' Mandy understood the
plan.

'Yes. Then I thought we might call in on the

Daveys,' Emily Hope continued as she pulled up and parked by the telephone box outside the post office.

'To see Mabel?' Mandy jumped out and ran round the back to open the door. She began to pull the badger's heavy cage towards her.

Her mum came to lend a hand. Together they lifted and carried the cage, Emily Hope walking backwards, Mandy guiding her across the pavement and down the narrow alley beside the stone-built post office. 'Yes, to see how Mabel's pregnancy is going,' Mrs Hope agreed. 'And to see Marmalade and—'

'Honey!' Mandy finished off. 'Careful! There's a patch of ice ahead.'

They skirted round the dangerous frozen puddle and carried on. Mandy's arms were aching, and the badger was turning anxiously inside the small space. His weight rocked the cage and made it more difficult to handle. In spite of the freezing cold, Mandy began to feel hot inside her thick jumper, jeans, boots and jacket.

'Nearly there,' Emily Hope said.

At last they reached the gate into the field and put the cage on the ground.

Mandy looked round. 'Watch out, there's someone coming!' she whispered. She could see in the moonlight that a solitary figure was crossing the frozen field.

'It's all right, it's only me!' The man waved and kept coming. 'I'm heading for my midweek pint at the pub.'

'Hello, David!' Emily Hope recognised the tall figure of David Gill, the owner of Greystones Farm. The far border of his land touched the copse where they planned to release the badger. She told him the plan and asked his advice. 'Are we doing the right thing, releasing the badger on his original home patch?'

'Quite right,' David Gill agreed. 'He'll soon see off any other creatures like foxes that might have moved in while he's been laid up in hospital, so to speak. Before you know it, it'll be business as usual for him.'

Mandy listened eagerly. 'Shall I let him out now?'

'Just wait for him to get his bearings.' Opening the wide gate into the field, the farmer explained that the badger would soon recognise where he was by familiar sounds and smells.

After a few minutes standing in a cold wind, blowing into their cupped hands and hugging themselves to keep warm, he said it was safe to open the door.

Mandy stooped and fumbled at the catch with her cold fingers. It clicked. The door swung open on its hinges and she stood back.

Cautiously the badger crept forward. At the edge of the cage he lowered his head and sniffed at the ground. He took one step out, then another, raising his head to look at the moon and stars: listening, watching.

'Go on!' Mandy urged him away from the road towards the open field. The knot in her stomach tightened.

The stripe of white along the sturdy creature's head showed clearly in the dim light. There was a gleam in his black eyes. Slowly he put his nose to the ground and snuffled towards the gate. His heavy paws crackled on the frosty grass. Then, with a sudden flurry and a push from his strong back legs, he was away.

Across the field, making a dark track through the white frost, the badger ran, silent, fast and low. He brushed past high tussocks of frozen grass and weeds, zigzagging past brambles until

he reached the bare hawthorn hedge by the wood. Then he stopped to look over his shoulder to where David Gill, Mandy and her mum still stood. There was a flash of white fur as he turned his head. Then he dipped low and crept through a break in the spiked branches, vanishing into the darkness.

'What did I tell you?' Mr Gill nodded and gave a satisfied grunt. 'He'll be right as rain from now on. And I'll get my lad, Brandon, to check out the sett every so often, just to make sure.'

Mandy smiled and sighed. She felt relieved and sad as the badger disappeared.

'Come on,' her mum said quietly. 'Let's go and see if the Daveys will give us a nice hot cup of tea.'

'Meet Marmalade, the cinnamon-coloured angora!' Joanna Davey introduced Mandy to a beautiful, silky-haired, bright orange creature. She held him in the palm of one hand, turned him on his back and tickled his white tummy.

'And this is Honey, a cream satin-coat.' John Davey showed her a trimmer, sleeker, pale fawn hamster with big dark eyes.

Mandy was thrilled to be handling the two cute, cheeky creatures at long last. They were every bit as adorable as she'd imagined during the long, nerve-wracking rehearsals for the Christmas play.

'She and Marmalade have been kept in the living-room while Mabel's been ill,' Mr Davey went on. 'They love the warmth from the fire, and now we haven't the heart to move them out to the breakfast-room again.'

John was obviously as keen on keeping fit as his athletic-looking wife. He wore jogging pants and trainers, with a bright red sweatshirt. His mid-brown hair was cut short, and his face glowed as if he'd just come back from a run.

'Would you like to hold Honey?' he said to Mandy.

She took the tiny creature and felt the hard claws and long, soft whiskers tickle her palm. She cupped her hands carefully, scared that Honey would take fright at being held by a stranger and try a kamikaze jump to freedom.

Meanwhile, Emily Hope was telling Joanna about the safe return of the badger to the wild. 'We fed him up while we had him at Animal Ark,' she told her, 'so he's laid down a couple of layers of fat as protection against the cold. We're hoping he'll find his old sett and be able to bed down there until the frost thaws.'

'The forecast is for snow this weekend,' Joanna reported.

'Good!' Mandy breathed.

'Are you hoping for a white Christmas?' John said, taking Honey back and putting her into her small plastic cage.

'No. I'm hoping they'll cancel the school show!' She explained about being press-ganged into being the Witch of the Sea.

'But we've bought tickets for that,' their new friend protested. 'We thought we'd go to the show as a way of getting to meet people.'

'We'll see you there, then.' Emily Hope watched Joanna return Marmalade to his cosy bed of wood shavings. Then they all went through to the breakfast-room to look at Mabel.

'All being well,' said John.

The grown-ups chatted while Mandy concentrated on Mabel, who looked cheerful and perky after her recent slight chill. The tubby, obviously pregnant white hamster was chewing at a dish of sunflower and sesame seeds, stuffing the food into her cheek pouches and glancing warily at Mandy all the while.

Emily Hope joined Mandy to cast an expert eye over the patient. 'How's the mum-to-be?' she asked.

'Thriving now.' John gave an update. 'Her babies are due on Saturday or Sunday, which is why I was a bit cautious about coming to the show on Monday night. It will depend on whether Mabel gives birth on the right day. If not, we might have to stick around to keep an eye on her.'

'Or you could go to the show, and I could stay with the hamster,' Joanna suggested. She had gone through to the kitchen to make a pot of tea.

'We'll see.'

Once more, Mandy let the conversation flow over her. She sat with her elbows on the table, watching Mabel pick at the seeds with her delicate paws, turning them this way and that, then stuffing them into her mouth. She thought of the badger rooting through the frosty undergrowth, announcing his return to the area with gruff barks and strong scents, scaring off any small creature who might have crept into his warm, well-built sett while he'd been away.

'Mandy?' Her mum's voice broke in.

'Mmm?' Mabel had finished her supper and was resting in her dark, warm nest-box. Mandy was gazing sleepily at what looked like an empty cage.

'Time to go.'

They said goodbye to the Daveys and drove home. Snowflakes began to drift across the headlight beams.

'Tired?' Emily Hope asked gently.

'Mmm,' Mandy nodded. 'Mabel's sweet. And so are Honey and Marmalade.'

'The show will soon be over,' her mum added sympathetically, turning carefully into the drive at Animal Ark. The lights in the house were switched on, casting a warm glow. There was a sprinkling of snow on the yard. 'And then it'll be Christmas and we can all relax!'

Five

'Still nervous?' Adam Hope asked Mandy as he drew up outside school on the Monday evening of the last week of term.

'Terrified,' she admitted.

The big night had arrived, but not the hoped-for snow. In fact, the weather had been cold and clear for days, and though a deep frost had set in, there wasn't a snow cloud to be seen.

Members of 'The Little Mermaid' cast and musicians in the Walton School orchestra had been able to travel freely to rehearsals from the villages and farms. The show had come together

in a last frantic scramble of costume-sewing,
scenery-painting and prop-making, so that by
the end of Sunday afternoon even Mrs Winterton
was satisfied that the show was going to be a
success.

'Remember, everyone, our school has a great
tradition of excellent Christmas shows to keep
up!' On the Sunday, she'd made a final speech
before they'd all trudged off home. 'I know the
orchestra will perform well, and every actor will
try to be word-perfect. Singers and dancers,
don't let me down. I know you can all do it,
each and every one of you!' The dark-haired
director had tried to be encouraging.

Daniel Winterton had sat at the back of the
hall as usual. All week, since Henry had ended
his adventures inside an empty violin case, the
little boy had kept in the background. Mandy
had found him hunched in corners over another
of his red notebooks. She would ask to look at
his story and try to be kind, but Daniel had
shaken his head and turned his back. Once or
twice, she'd found him in the biology lab,
drawing pictures of Henry and sticking them in
his book. But when he'd noticed her, Daniel
had slipped out without a word.

'I bet Daniel will be glad when the show's over,' James had said as they all trooped out of school on the Sunday evening. The dress-rehearsal had been long and tiring. He too had noticed how unhappy the little boy had been.

'He's not the only one,' Mandy had sighed. 'You know something? I'd rather have a week of non-stop maths lessons than do this show!'

'I'd rather . . . walk a tightrope across Niagara Falls!' James had declared.

'Or get stuck in a lift with . . . Mrs Ponsonby!' Mandy struggled to invent fates worse than death.

'What's that about our dear Mrs P?' Adam Hope had asked, holding open the Land-rover door for James and Mandy to climb in.

'Nothing!' they'd said together, sinking back into the seats.

But neither Mandy nor James had slept a wink that night, and all day at school, the tension had mounted.

'I wish I could make time stand still!' James had whispered to Mandy when he'd seen her in the corridor at lunch-time.

'Maybe we could break an arm or a leg!' She'd suggested the rash solution after school, as they waited for the bus to take them home to Welford. 'Then we wouldn't be able to take part.'

But their sensible mums had made an early tea and made sure they were ready for the big night.

'Good luck!' Emily Hope had called from the doorstep of Animal Ark, as a pale-faced, trembling Mandy had set off back to school. 'I'll see you later!'

Adam Hope had collected James and driven them over the moor, and now here they were standing in the school entrance with dozens of other nervous actors, musicians and dancers. 'Watch out, here comes the boss!' he murmured with a grin, as Mrs Winterton strode across the carpark, trailing Daniel after her. The music teacher looked as nervous and on edge as any member of her cast.

'Not now, Daniel!' she insisted.

'But, Mu-um!' It seemed to Mandy that he'd been pestering for some time. His voice was whining and pathetic; his mother's mouth was set in a firm line. 'Why can't I have another hamster? You said I could have a treat if I was good. And I have been, haven't I? I've been really, really quiet and I haven't got in your way at all this week!'

Trotting in his mother's footsteps, the little boy didn't seem to realise that he'd chosen the worst possible moment to ask. Mandy felt sorry for him and shrugged her shoulders at her dad and James. Then they all stood to one side as Mrs Winterton swept by.

'And I will look after it, I promise! I'll feed it and clean it and make sure it gets plenty of exercise!'

Mrs Winterton stopped inside the porch, clutching her music scores and bending forward to hiss in his ear. 'Daniel, will you listen to me? I'm very, very busy right now. The last thing I want to think about is whether or not you can keep another smelly little hamster in the house!'

'Hamsters aren't smelly,' he protested stubbornly, staring up at her without blinking. 'And you said I could choose my favourite treat!'

'But *not* a hamster!' She put her face close to his. Their noses were only centimetres apart, Daniel's eyes wide and blank, his mother's blazing with frustration. 'Do you understand? I'm busy. I'm trying to put on a show!'

Adam Hope cleared his throat and stepped

forward. 'Would you like me to take Daniel out for a little while?' he offered.

'Aha!' Mrs Winterton seized his arm. 'Now, Daniel, Mandy's father is a vet. He'll tell you exactly why we can't have another hamster, then that will be the end of it!'

'I will?' Adam Hope looked surprised.

'Yes, tell him that they take an awful lot of looking after.'

'Erm . . . as a matter of fact . . .'

Mandy listened to her dad stammer and tail off. Mrs Winterton was determined to have her say.

'And anyway, Daniel, remember what it was like when Norvik died!' She turned to Mr Hope. 'To be honest, I didn't really have anything to do with the creature – I'm not keen on rodents, so Daniel's father took care of it. But Daniel doted on it. He was absolutely heartbroken when we lost it, and cried for days.'

'It can be a very upsetting experience,' Adam Hope admitted thoughtfully.

'He moped and moped,' Daniel's mother continued, 'then started writing these adventure stories. Really, I was quite worried about him for weeks afterwards!'

'But Dad isn't away *all* of the time,' Daniel muttered. 'If we got another hamster, he could help me look after him again. And anyway, I'm older. I can do it myself, now.'

His mother shook her head. 'You see what I mean!' She appealed to Mandy's father. 'He's obsessed with hamsters.'

'Let me look after him for half an hour,' Adam Hope offered again. 'I have to drive back to Welford to pick up Mandy's mother and grandparents. Daniel could come along for the ride.'

The music teacher looked at her watch and nodded. 'Thanks. That would be nice, wouldn't it, Daniel?'

'Hmm,' the boy grunted, then looked away, out at the frost-covered carpark and the row of holly trees beyond.

Mr Hope shrugged at Mandy and wished her and James luck before they rushed off to get ready for the show. 'Knock 'em dead!' he said with a wink.

Mandy swallowed hard. Her throat was already dry, her palms sticky, and there was still an hour to go before the curtain went up.

'And, Daniel, before we go on our drive, why

don't you take me to see the school hamster?'
Mr Hope spoke casually, but gave Mrs Winterton
a serious look. 'You could show me how Henry's
getting on, couldn't you?'

Daniel's face lit up at the word 'hamster'. He
glowed when he heard Mr Hope say 'Henry'.

But Mrs Winterton didn't like the idea. 'No,'
she said with a firm shake of her head. 'I'd
rather you didn't encourage him.'

So Adam Hope swiftly changed tack. 'OK,
then. Daniel, are you ready to set off right away?'

The little boy stared at the floor in silence.

'Daniel?' his mother prompted.

'Yes,' said a small, flat voice. Daniel hung his
head as Mr Hope explained that they would be
back in time for the show.

'So, Mandy, get a move on,' Mrs Winterton
ordered, noticing her hovering nearby. 'I want
everyone in costume by seven o'clock. That
gives you exactly twenty minutes to get changed
and made up. And you, James, hurry up! There
isn't a moment to lose!'

The first-floor room where the cast changed
into costume overlooked the school's main
entrance. Mandy dashed up there in time to

see her dad and Daniel driving out of the grounds past the row of tall holly trees. She sighed, then went to find Miss Temple, who gave her the flowing black costume and tall witch's hat.

'I want you to wear these for the actual performance,' the biology teacher told her, handing Mandy a set of small, greenish plastic objects. 'They're Hallowe'en witch's fingernails – just right for the part.'

Mandy stuck one on the end of each finger and wiggled them. Now her hands really did look witchlike.

'And you didn't have full green make-up on for the dress-rehearsal, did you?' Miss Temple sat Mandy down on a stool and slapped on the cold, oily-smelling theatre panstick. 'And wrinkles.' A black eyebrow pencil made lines between Mandy's eyes and down the sides of her mouth.

Mandy held still while the teacher worked. At the end of the session, when she looked in the mirror with her blacked-out front teeth and wispy grey wig under the tall hat, she hardly recognised herself.

'Now wait quietly for curtain-up,' Miss

Temple told her, moving on to Susan Collins. 'And don't smudge your wrinkles!'

Mandy raised her arms and wriggled her witch-fingers in front of the mirror. She mimed a cackle. *Hmm, not bad.* She twirled round in her floating, flowing black cape. *Not bad at all.* 'Like my fingernails?' she asked James, who had just got changed into his courtier's costume.

'Mandy?' He stared at her doubtfully.

'Yes, it's me!' She gave a toothless grin.

'Hey!' he said, obviously impressed.

Then she went to look out of the window at the cars arriving for the show, wondering if her dad had come back with her mum and her grandparents.

James followed. 'Here come Simon and Jean,' he pointed out.

Simon was the young nurse at Animal Ark, and he'd given the receptionist a lift from Welford. The two of them walked together to join a steady flow into the building.

'And Mr and Mrs Collins.' Mandy pointed out a sleek, shiny car. Getting out were Susan's glamorous actress-mother and tall, smart-looking father. Mrs Collins was wrapped in a warm fur coat, with a white silk scarf thrown across one shoulder. 'I hope that fur's fake,' Mandy grumbled, enjoying her bird's-eye view.

'Course it is!' Susan said in passing. She was wearing her long mermaid's wig and tight, shiny fish-tail, taking tiny steps across the room. 'Mummy wouldn't wear real fur!'

'That was Susan Collins!' Mandy mouthed at James, in case he hadn't recognised the star of the show.

'I know!' He pointed out more new arrivals. 'Ernie Bell and Walter Pickard . . . Mrs Ponsonby with Marjorie and Joan Spry . . .'

Mandy glanced down at the three old ladies. Mrs Ponsonby was dressed in a red cape and hat. She carried Pandora under one arm and held Toby's lead with the other hand. She was stopped at the door by Mr Browning, who seemed to be explaining that dogs weren't allowed in the school building. Mrs Ponsonby protested. The caretaker stood firm. So while the Spry twins went in to take their seats in the hall, a fuming Mrs Ponsonby was forced to take her precious pets back to the car.

'I hope they're going to be warm enough.' Mandy watched closely as the old lady settled them down in a nest of blankets in the back of

her car, which was parked in the shelter of the
holly bushes. She opened a window for fresh air
and wagged her finger at Toby to warn him to
be good. Then, satisfied that the dogs would be
all right, she bustled back towards the main
entrance.

'Five minutes to go!' James looked at the clock
above the door.

Mandy's stomach lurched. She was trying not
to think about curtain-up.

'Here come the McKays.' James had spotted
his Welford neighbours: Dr and Mrs McKay and
their daughter, Claire. They ran Rosa's Refuge,
the hedgehog sanctuary, from the back garden
of their large house. People were arriving thick
and fast. 'Three minutes!' he murmured.

Mandy felt her skin begin to prickle and sweat
form under the thick layer of make-up. 'I'm
going to melt!' she groaned. Suddenly, she had
a panic. 'Where's Dad got to?' The whole of
Welford seemed to be here, except for her
family.

'Would all members of the orchestra please
take their places in the hall!' Mrs Winterton
called from the dressing-room door. Her voice
was high and tense as the big moment drew near.

The room emptied as the musicians took their instruments and filed downstairs.

'And all actors and dancers for the opening scene, please make your way backstage!' The music teacher checked their costumes as they passed. 'You look lovely, Susan!' She tweaked the mermaid's wig and shiny fish scales, then sent her on her way.

'Mandy, I have to go. Are you OK?' James asked.

'Yep.' She gazed anxiously out of the window. Her first appearance wasn't until Scene Two.

'If it's your dad you're worried about, I'm sure he'll turn up.' He was reluctant to leave, but Mrs Winterton was waiting impatiently at the door. 'See you later.'

'Good luck!' she told him absent-mindedly. Where could her family have got to? Would they all miss the beginning of the show?

'You too,' James murmured, leaving her alone.

All this, and Mum, Dad, Gran and Grandad might not even be here to see her! Mandy tried not to let disappointment get the better of her. *There must be a good reason*, she told herself.

They've just been held up for a little while. They'll be here soon.

Gazing out of the window, down at the rows of parked cars, she saw nothing but the shadows of the holly trees falling long and silent across the frost-covered drive.

Six

'Hello up there!' A faint call from the carpark distracted Mandy's attention from the silent trees. 'Witch of the Sea – Mandy Hope! Hello!'

It was her gran, standing by the Animal Ark Land-rover which had just driven into the school grounds. She was waving her arms and smiling up at Mandy, who opened the window and leaned out. 'You're here!' she cried.

'Sorry we're late, love. The show hasn't started yet, has it?' Dorothy Hope stepped to one side to let Mandy's grandad, Emily Hope and Daniel Winterton out of the car. The grown-ups looked flustered, but Daniel was beaming all over his face.

'Not quite.' Mandy glanced up at the clock. 'One minute to go!'

'There was a small crisis at the Daveys' house on our way here. I wonder, is there any room at the inn for two unexpected visitors?' Gran called.

Mystified, Mandy leaned still further out. 'What do you mean?'

'Come and see!' Dorothy Hope beckoned her down.

'Can I, please?' Mandy turned to ask Miss Temple, who had come to join her at the window. Apart from the two of them, the room was empty.

'Let's both go,' the teacher decided promptly, taking in the situation and heading for the door. 'We'll use the back stairs, then no latecomers will catch sight of you in costume.'

They slipped quickly along the corridor, down to the ground floor, past the art room and into Miss Temple's biology lab.

Mandy flew across the room ahead of the teacher, her black robes billowing behind her. Out of the corner of her eye, she glimpsed

Henry in his cage. The hamster was sitting quietly at his food dish. Mandy pushed open the side door that led on to the sloping path and was greeted by a blast of freezing cold air.

Quickly, she and Miss Temple ran up the frosty path, Mandy knocking snow off the holly trees and brushing against low branches as she rushed by. The snow slid from the shiny leaves and fell with a soft thud.

'Mandy, there you are! That's a marvellous costume, dear!' Gran greeted her as she rounded the corner. 'We're late because your mum decided to call in on the Daveys to see if they wanted to follow us over the moor in their car, and it's a good job she did!'

'Why? What happened?' Mandy was about to give her gran a quick hug, but remembered her straggly wig and greasy make-up and, held back.

'Hi, Grandad! What's wrong?'

'Whoa!' Tom Hope saw her for the first time. 'You nearly frightened me out of my wits!' He gave Mandy an admiring grin before taking a square box covered in a cloth from Emily Hope. Mandy's mum took a second, similar box from the Land-rover and gave it to the still-beaming Daniel. Then Gran closed the door.

'Now, no need to worry,' Mandy's kindly grandfather reassured her and Miss Temple. 'But, as Dorothy said, what we need is a nice, warm, quiet place for two little unexpected visitors!'

'What *kind* of visitors?' Mandy gathered her cloak around her. The cold and stage fright were both making her shiver. Her teeth began to chatter in the icy wind.

'Hamsters!' Daniel said with a bright grin.

'Honey and Marmalade,' Adam Hope told her, coming round from the driver's side. 'Can you find somewhere for us to put them while we go in and watch the show?'

Mandy stared at the two covered boxes in Daniel's and her grandad's arms. For a few seconds she was too surprised to answer, but now she saw what her gran had meant by 'room at the inn'.

Miss Temple stepped in. 'Bring them to the lab. Follow me.' Quickly she retraced her steps down the side path.

'How come?' Mandy gathered her wits and trotted alongside Daniel. Everyone was following the biology teacher in a tight crocodile. From inside the building, sounds of the orchestra tuning up drifted out.

'We got to the Daveys' house just as Mabel decided to give birth. A real coincidence, you have to admit.' Adam Hope continued the explanation.

'I thought the babies were due at the weekend.' Mandy ran to hold the lab door open. Daniel, her gran, grandad, mum and dad followed the teacher out of the cold.

'They were, but they were late. As it turned out, the birth was complicated, so it was a good job we were there.'

'Your mum and dad saved their lives!' Daniel said. He carried the hamster cage with great care.

'Poor little Mabel had gone into labour,' Gran continued, 'but the first baby was stuck upside-down in the birth canal. The mother hamster needed help to deliver him, then all the others could follow safely.'

'It was brilliant!' Daniel added.

'How many?' Mandy asked. She pictured the scene.

'Six,' Tom Hope reported, putting the first cage down on the shelf next to Henry, where Miss Temple had shown him. He took off the cover and leaned forward to check that Marmalade was OK. 'Six bright pink, naked, tiny, wriggling creatures. Completely helpless.'

'Fantastic!' Daniel insisted, breathless with wonder.

Mandy gasped. 'How are they? How's Mabel?'

Grandad turned to the experts.

'Doing quite well,' Emily Hope replied cautiously. She took Honey's cage from the boy and gently put it on the shelf. As she lifted the cover, they saw a furry cream face nuzzling up to the wire mesh, peering curiously at her new surroundings. 'But Mabel was exhausted after the difficult birth, and the babies are weak. Joanna and John will have to help the mother look after them for the first couple of days, and that will keep them very busy.'

'So meanwhile, because they had their hands full, we offered to babysit these two cheeky little things at Lilac Cottage.' Grandad grinned at Honey and Marmalade.

Dorothy Hope quickly finished off the story. 'The only trouble was, we were already late for the show. So we decided to bring the hamsters with us!'

Down the corridor in the main hall, the

orchestra was a few minutes late in striking up the opening number.

'It sounds like we're going to miss the beginning after all.' Adam Hope heard the music and sighed.

'No. If you're quick, you can still make it!' Miss Temple hurried them through the door in a jumble of jostling arms and legs. 'Don't worry, the hamsters will be quite safe on Henry's shelf. We'll keep an eye on them for you!'

Emily Hope closed the lab door behind her. She turned to smile at Mandy. 'Good luck!' she whispered. 'And by the way, love, you look amazing. I'm sure you're going to be absolutely fine!'

Mandy stood in the wings, waiting for her first entrance. She watched the scene-shifters roll her house, supposedly made from the bones of shipwrecked men, into position in the middle of the stage. The house had been painted by some of the older pupils in the school, and the effect was very eerie.

As the stage assistants had finished, a green light glowed on the witch's house, and spooky music began to play.

Mandy closed her eyes. *Please let me remember my lines!* Her throat was dry, her tongue stuck to the roof of her mouth, and her knees shook.

'You'll be OK.' James stood at her shoulder, encouraging her. He'd appeared in the first scene and lived to tell the tale. 'Once you get out there, it's not too bad.'

She swallowed hard. The musical build-up to the witch's entrance grew louder. Down there in the front row, her parents and grandparents sat expectantly.

Thirty seconds more, and she would be under the spotlight with Susan Collins, speaking her first words.

But suddenly, out of nowhere, Daniel Winterton flashed into her mind. 'Oh no!' she gasped, staring at a gap in the front row of seats. It could only mean one thing.

'What?' James stared at her as if she'd gone mad, his glasses glinting green from a reflection of the overhead lights.

'Daniel's not in his seat!'

'So?' James turned her round to face the stage. Any second now, the cymbals would clash and Mandy would have to make her entrance.

'He's up to something!' Mandy gabbled. 'I

don't know what, but now I come to think of it, I didn't see him leave the biology lab with the rest of us. He's could still be in there with Henry! And Honey and Marmalade!'

'Mandy, what are you on about?' James spread his hands helplessly.

'I don't know exactly!' she hissed. The cymbals clashed. She clenched her fists and got ready to enter. 'But I've got this strange feeling!'

'Stage fright,' he muttered.

'No. James, I'm worried about the hamsters!' *Crash-clash-rumble!* That was Mandy's cue.

'OK, I'll go and check,' he promised as Mandy swooped on stage.

The green light flashed purple and there was a mighty drum-roll.

' "I already know what you want!" ' Mandy said with a horrible cackle. ' "You want to get rid of your fish-tail and have two stumps to walk on like human beings. It is very stupid of you!" '

She heard the children in the audience gasp at her green face and long, pointed fingernails. Whirling her cloak about her, making the paper snakes squirm across the stage, Mandy forgot for the moment all about James, Daniel Winterton and the three furry hamsters.

Seven

The Witch of the Sea told the Little Mermaid that she would grant her wish. Eerie music played as she mixed a magic potion. Then she whirled her black cloak around her with a cackle. '*Waagh-haagh-haagh-ha-ha-ha-haagh!*' The stage lights flashed green and purple, and the scene ended on a roll of drums and screech of violins.

'Phew!' Mandy was off-stage, standing in the wings with Susan, amazed that she'd made it. Her legs felt like jelly.

'You were great!' Susan grinned at her,

pausing before she hurried off to change her costume.

'Really?' It had all happened in a blur of overhead lights and loud music.

'Yes, really!'

The next scene was already underway. Mandy wouldn't be needed again for at least fifteen minutes, so she made her way along the ground-floor corridor, hearing the music fade into the distance as she went looking for James.

'Mandy!' He appeared at the biology lab door.

'What's wrong?' She could tell in an instant that James had bad news. He was beckoning her to hurry, but keeping his voice low.

'What are all these hamster cages doing here?'

Mandy realised that she hadn't had time to fill James in on the latest events. She tried to explain as quickly as she could, then move on to her worries about Daniel. But he cut her short.

'OK, OK, I get the picture. And you were right to send me to check,' he told her, pulling her in through the door and closing it after her. 'Come and look!'

Across the room, the three hamster cages sat side by side on the shelf. Inside one, Mandy saw Henry trundling happily inside his wheel, spinning it fast, almost as if showing off in front of his visitors. His pink ears were laid flat against his head, his feet scrabbled at the rungs, and his little backside swayed as he ran.

Then she looked in the next cage. Marmalade, the Daveys' long-haired, cinnamon-coloured hamster, had his face pressed eagerly against the bars of his cage. His nose was squashed flat and his whiskers poked through, as if pleading to be let out to play.

But then Mandy looked at the third cage. There was a pile of wood shavings in one corner, a plastic tube for Honey to play with in another. The food dish at the front of the cage had been upturned and the seeds and nuts scattered across the floor. But there was no silky fawn creature with bright black eyes peering out, no Honey picking at the spilt food with dainty paws . . . nothing . . . no hamster in there at all!

'Where's Honey? Where's Daniel?' Mandy spun round. Her fears seemed to be confirmed.

'Search me!' James stood by helpless as the news sank in. 'He wasn't here when I arrived, and neither was what-do-you-call-her . . . Honey.'

He took off his glasses and wiped them on his shirt, giving himself thinking time. 'You don't suppose Daniel's stolen her, do you?'

Mandy searched the shelf, behind stacks of books and packets of hamster food. She remembered the last time Henry had vanished. 'He wouldn't . . . would he?'

'You know how mad he is about hamsters.' James obviously thought they had to consider the possibility. 'And you said you thought you'd left him in here.'

Mandy sighed and gave up her search along the shelf. 'He was really disappointed when Mrs Winterton told him he couldn't have another one.' Her stomach was beginning to flutter as it began to appear more likely that the unhappy little boy had done something really silly this time. 'We have to talk to him!' she decided.

'How long have you got before your next entrance?' James asked, taking one last look through the bars at the empty cage.

'About twelve minutes. How about you?'

James looked at his watch. 'Six.'

Enough time to find Daniel and ask him if he knows anything about Honey. 'Let's try the side door,' Mandy suggested, darting between the workbenches to push hard at the handle. Two of her witch's fingernails came loose and fell off.

'Locked,' James told her, stooping to pick them up. 'I've already tried it.'

Miss Temple or Mr Browning must have made sure that the building was secure after they'd brought the cages in through the side door. 'Good. At least Daniel can't have stolen Honey and dashed outside into the cold with her.'

'*If*!' James insisted, trying not to jump to conclusions. '*If* he has stolen her.'

'OK.' After the shock of finding Honey gone, Mandy began to calm down. She took a deep breath. 'Let's think. Daniel probably stayed down here when we left the lab.' She began to count points off on her fingers. 'So he must have hidden somewhere here, and waited until everyone had left . . .' She was so busy thinking out loud, she didn't notice James's frown as his attention switched to Miss Temple's storeroom. There seemed to be a noise coming from inside.

'Shh!' He raised his finger to his lips.

Mandy stopped suddenly. She strained to hear.

On the wall above the door, the clock ticked

loudly. In the distance, the orchestra played and the choir sang.

'Did you hear that?' James crept softly towards the storeroom door. 'Someone's crying.'

She followed and watched him listen at the closed door. Yes, there was a muffled sob and a sniff.

'Daniel?' James asked, trying the handle. 'Don't scare him,' he warned Mandy.

'What do you mean?' she hissed. Did he think she was going to rush in and pounce?

'Your costume!' James pointed out. 'You even scare *me* in that!'

'Oh, it's OK. Daniel saw me in costume when he arrived with the hamsters,' she explained.

James nodded. 'Daniel? It's us, James and Mandy. Can we come in?'

There was another sob, a louder sniffle. 'Honey's lost!' a tearful voice wailed. 'But I didn't steal her! It's not my fault!'

'Listen, Daniel, come out so we can talk.' James spoke as if they had plenty of time. He sounded calm and patient as he peered in through the frosted glass panel. 'Or will you let us come in there?'

'I'll come out,' Daniel answered miserably. He

appeared at the door, his round face tear-stained, his eyes red. As turned the handle, the storeroom door swung open and he spotted Mandy. He gasped and took a quick step back.

'It's me!' she assured him. 'Remember?' She took off her hat and wig, then shook out her blonde hair. 'Did you know Honey had gone missing?'

The little boy nodded. 'But it wasn't me!'

'So you don't know where she is?' Mandy couldn't help feeling suspicious. She narrowed her eyes and stared at Daniel.

'No!' he protested. Tears came back into his eyes.

'But no one else has been in the lab, have they?' Mandy felt the seconds ticking by. Soon James would have to go back on stage. At this rate, she would have to start the search for Honey by herself.

'No,' Daniel admitted, hanging his head. 'But I never stole her!'

'OK, we believe you. But we don't understand what's happened.' The less time they had, the more patient James seemed. He led the way across the room towards the three hamster cages.

As Daniel looked up at the empty cage, his lip began to tremble.

'Are you telling us that you didn't go anywhere near Honey's cage?' James pressed him carefully.

'I never said that. I said I never stole her, even if that's what everyone thinks!'

James raised his eyebrows and glanced at Mandy. 'Right, so you did go up to her cage?'

Without waiting for Daniel's answer, Mandy seized the opening. 'Did you want to play with her?'

The little boy looked down at the floor and nodded. 'Just for a minute.'

'So you opened the cage and took her out?'

There was a long silence. Daniel shuffled his feet and sniffed. Then he nodded.

'But you did put her back?' Mandy wanted to believe him. 'This was an accident, wasn't it? Honey wasn't meant to escape.' Inside their cages, Henry and Marmalade scuffed and scuttled.

'I only played with her,' Daniel murmured.

James glanced at the clock over the door. 'And what happened after you put her back in the cage?'

Daniel shrugged.

'Come on, Daniel. This is really important,' Mandy urged. They needed every single clue they could get to start the search for the Daveys' missing hamster. 'Show us what you did.'

Sighing, Mrs Winterton's son dragged a stool underneath the shelf and climbed on to it. 'I held her carefully and lifted the door, like this.'

Honey's cage door had a hinge across the top. Daniel lifted the whole of the front to show them how it worked.

Mandy nodded. 'Then you put her inside?'

He nodded. 'I put some crisps in her food bowl. She loves crisps! She was so greedy, she knocked the bowl over while I was shutting the door.' He showed them how he'd done this, then climbed down from the stool.

'Wait!' James said. 'Show us how you fixed the latch on the door.

'Like this.' Daniel reached up and clumsily twisted the metal latch with his stubby fingers. He left it without managing to secure the door firmly in place.

Mandy's eyebrows shot up and she drew a deep breath. So this was how Honey had escaped! The clock's minute hand jerked forward. 'Then where did you go?' she asked Daniel.

He frowned. 'I went to Mum's locker to get Honey some more crisps from my bag,' he told them. 'There was enough to go round; some for her, and some for Henry and Marmalade. I only left them alone for a few minutes. But when I came back, the cage was empty. Honey had gone!'

'Don't tell Mum!' Daniel had pleaded. He'd begun to sob all over again as he realised what he'd done.

James had been forced to leave Mandy and Daniel in the lab and dash back for his next scene in the show. He'd promised to come back in ten more minutes to spend the interval looking for the escaped hamster.

'We can't tell her, can we?' Mandy told the little boy, offering him the edge of her cloak to wipe away his tears. 'She's out in front of the stage, conducting the orchestra, so don't worry about that just yet.'

'I never meant it.'

'We know that. It was an accident. But Daniel, Mr and Mrs Davey will be really upset, so we have to do our very best to find Honey before they hear about it, OK?'

He dried his eyes and nodded.

'Because something like this could ruin Christmas for them,' she explained. 'And my gran and grandad promised to take good care of Honey, so they'll feel sad that they've let them down, and that could spoil their Christmas too.'

'I'm sorry,' Daniel murmured. He stared at Mandy with his big, round, sad eyes.

She nodded back. 'So I'm going to leave you here in the lab with the door closed, while I go back and do the witch's scene. You have to look everywhere. Find Honey for us.'

Daniel lifted his chin and jutted it out. 'I'll try,' he promised.

'And you know those crisps you went to fetch? You could use one or two to tempt Honey out. If she's hiding behind a cupboard and she smells her favourite food, she might creep out for a quick snack. That's when you could catch her and put her back in her cage. Gently. Don't hurt her.' Taking her example from James, Mandy tried hard to sound calmer than she felt.

'OK.' Daniel took the packet from his pocket and scattered one or two crisps on the workbench below Honey's cage. Inside their own cages, Henry and Marmalade twitched the tips of their noses. Food!

Mandy took one last look around the room at the teacher's desk and blackboard, the stacks of books, the wallcharts and rows of benches. 'Don't open the other two cages, whatever you do,' she told Daniel. 'And don't open the lab door to anyone except James. It's the half-time interval after this next scene, so James and I will be back as soon as we can.'

He nodded nervously. 'Don't be long.'

As she turned the door handle, she could hear the music building up to her next entrance. Everyone backstage would be frantically looking for the Witch of the Sea. 'I've got to go!' She only had time for one final reassurance. 'Don't worry, Daniel. Honey can't have gone far!'

'At least I hope not,' Mandy muttered to herself as she slipped from the room, jamming her wig and hat on to her head as she sped along the corridor. There was no guarantee that Honey would be easy to find in this maze of strange corridors and classrooms.

As she dashed on stage under green and purple flashing lights, Mandy knew that the tiny honey-coloured hamster could be absolutely anywhere in the school!

Eight

'Daniel, would you let us in, please?' Adam Hope was tapping at the biology lab door.

Mandy had whooshed off stage in a cloud of dry-ice smoke, giving her best cackle yet. The curtain had come down and it was time for interval tea and biscuits.

While the audience had gathered for refreshments in the home economics room, she'd dashed back to the lab to help Daniel find the missing hamster. But here were her mum and dad knocking at the door and peering anxiously through the glass pane.

Emily Hope saw Mandy flying down the corridor, her cloak wafting behind her. 'Who needs a broomstick?' she joked.

'Hey, Mandy, you're terrific!' Adam Hope glanced round but kept on tapping at the door. 'This is odd. Your mum decided to come and check on the Daveys' hamsters, and we know that Daniel is in there. We saw him before he noticed us. He's jammed a stool against the door and is down on his hands and knees, obviously looking for something that he's lost.'

Mandy's mum pulled a face, then stared carefully at Mandy. 'You don't happen to know what's going on by any chance?'

Mandy sighed. 'I told him not to let anyone in,' she confessed.

Just then, James came running round the corner by the lockers and cloakrooms. 'Sorry, I got held up,' he gasped. He stopped short when he saw Mr and Mrs Hope.

'It's the hamsters, isn't it?' Emily Hope said quietly, looking from James to Mandy and back again.

'Honey,' Mandy agreed. Quickly she told them the whole story, watching a frown develop on her mum's pretty, freckled face.

Her dad scratched his beard thoughtfully. 'I knew Daniel was longing for Mrs Winterton to give in and agree to have another hamster, and I felt that perhaps he wasn't quite old enough to look after one by himself just yet. I suppose this proves the point.'

'What do we do now?' James went forward to peer through the door. 'I can see Honey's cage from here, and it's definitely still empty.'

'Daniel must be too scared to open up.' Mandy craned her neck to see. She spotted a pair of trainers sticking out from under one of the benches, and two legs. The rest of the little boy's body was hidden by a cupboard. 'Daniel, it's OK!' She stooped to call through the keyhole. 'It's Mandy and James. Take the stool away and open the door.'

Slowly he crept out from under the bench. His face was pale, his eyes dark and frightened as he approached the door to let them in. 'Honey didn't come out of her hiding-place to eat the crisps,' he whispered sadly.

Mandy decided not to let him see how worried she was. 'Mum and Dad will help us look,' she told him as, one by one, they slipped into the lab.

Emily Hope went straight to the cage and checked it. 'Maybe I'd better get in touch with the Daveys and tell them what's happened.'

'Not yet.' Mandy's dad considered the problem. 'Wait until the end of the interval. You never know, Honey might show up once we all start looking. If not, we can ring Joanna and John and warn them then.'

'But I feel so responsible,' Mrs Hope sighed with a shake of her head. Her long red hair fell across her shoulders. 'I should have dropped Mum and Dad off and driven the hamsters back to Lilac Cottage instead of leaving them here during the show.'

'And missed Mandy's starring role?' Mr Hope pointed out. He did his best to make everyone feel better. 'Listen, Rather than blaming anyone, let's all set to and see if we can find the runaway.'

Mandy was the last one into the lab. She glanced up and down the corridor before she closed the door, hoping for Daniel's sake that his mother wouldn't come looking for him during the interval. But she felt her heart sink into her long, pointy witch's shoes when she saw the stout figure of Mrs Ponsonby sailing towards them.

'Quick!' Mandy tried to bundle James into the room.

'Yoo-hoo, Mandy!' A cloud of flowery perfume and a loud voice announced the arrival of the owner of Bleakfell Hall.

Too late! Mandy closed her eyes and grimaced.

'Adam, I'm so glad you're here!' Mrs Ponsonby cried, her scarlet velvet beret perched at a jaunty angle, her cream Pekinese dog peeking out from under her red cape. Somehow Pandora had escaped the caretaker's eagle eye. She pushed past Mandy and James, then launched herself into a booming explanation. 'I went out to take a custard cream each to Toby and Pandora, and lo and behold, I spied the Animal Ark Land-rover!'

'Erm, Mrs Ponsonby, I'm rather busy just now.' Mandy's dad tried to usher the old lady back towards the door.

Mandy saw Pandora reach out to nip his hand as he put it on Mrs Ponsonby's arm. Her dad snatched it away in the nick of time.

Blissfully unaware, Mrs Ponsonby stood her ground. 'When I saw your car, I said to myself, "Carpe diem. Seize the day!" You could say that was the Ponsonby family motto.'

'Pardon?' Adam Hope raised his eyebrows at Mandy and nodded for her and the others to continue the search for Honey while he dealt with Mrs Ponsonby as best he could.

'Seize the day! In other words, never miss an opportunity. Or, again, never put off until tomorrow what you can do today! And of course, we're coming up to Christmas, and I do want poor Pandora to be completely better by then!'

'Mrs Ponsonby, I'm afraid I don't know what you're talking about . . .'

Mandy heard her poor dad trying to cope as she went to the windows and began to raise the blinds to look behind them for a clue to Honey's whereabouts. Meanwhile, Emily Hope had taken Daniel off to look in the technicians' storeroom, and James was concentrating his search under the radiators and behind the teacher's desk.

'Pandora . . . sneezing . . . surely you haven't forgotten my visit to the surgery in the snow!' Mrs Ponsonby gave a whinnying laugh. 'Oh, Adam, you're teasing me. Of course you remember!'

'Erm . . . of course. How could I forget?'

Adam Hope coughed and stammered. 'But didn't we decide that Pandora had probably sniffed some pepper on the braised steak you'd given her as a special lunch-time treat?'

'Ah, yes!' The large lady broke in triumphantly. 'But she sneezed again this morning . . . three times. And this time she hadn't had any steak!'

'Ah!' Mr Hope half sighed, half groaned.

'I've been worried about her all day, and when I saw your car, I decided to seize the iron while it was hot!'

Making her way along the windowsills without success, Mandy bumped into James, who was looking for Honey under a radiator. He rolled his eyes and shook his head.

'Iron?' Mr Hope echoed faintly.

'Yes. I told Toby to be a good boy and stay in the car, and I brought Pandora inside for you to have a look at. And now the heavens have smiled on me, because I've found you straight away, so you have plenty of time to examine her before the show starts again!' The old lady set the Pekinese dog down on a workbench and hovered eagerly nearby.

'Any luck? James? Mandy?' Emily Hope poked

her head round the storeroom door to ask them how they were getting on.

They shook their heads and went on searching, while Adam Hope admitted defeat and began to examine a tetchy Pandora. Mandy joined James on her hands and knees, searching every centimetre of skirting-board round the walls to see if there was a small hole that an adventurous hamster might have slipped through. As she backed towards the door, she felt it open.

'Mandy?' Grandad's puzzled voice interrupted Pandora's low growls. 'What are you doing down there? What have you lost?'

Quick-witted Gran came in behind him. She took in the situation at a glance and went straight over to the empty hamster cage to confirm her suspicions. Immediately, she too began to search every corner of the room.

Grandad was slower to catch on. 'Why is this cage empty?' he queried, scratching his bald head. 'Don't tell me one of the Daveys' hamsters has made a run for it!'

'Shh, Grandad!' Mandy warned. If Mrs Ponsonby heard, soon all the world would know.

'Hamster?' Sharp-eared Mrs Ponsonby picked up the word. 'Gone missing? Don't tell me it's that charming little chap, Henry!'

Though Mrs Ponsonby hadn't always had a soft spot for hamsters, she'd taken to Henry when he'd found his way into a hamper full of food she'd been preparing at a caravan site the previous summer. Now she left Pandora to Mr Hope's tender mercies and rushed over to the three cages.

'Oh, there you are, Henry!' She spotted the golden-brown hamster peeking out of his cage and made tweeting noises with her lips. Then she went on in a sing-song voice, 'You wouldn't run away again, would you, dear?'

'Yuck!' Mandy squirmed with embarrassment.

'Oh, wouldn't he?' James muttered.

Mrs Ponsonby turned her attention to him. 'James, dear, don't mumble. I take it you and Mandy are looking for a different hamster? And did I hear the name "Davey" mentioned?' This time the bossy old lady swung round to confront Mandy's grandad. 'Isn't that the couple who've moved into the house next door to the post office?'

Soon she'd pieced the story together and begun to organise a search party to look further afield. 'Tom, see if you can delay the start of the second act until the hamster has been found,' she ordered.

'We can't do that!' Grandad objected.

Mrs Ponsonby waved her hand impatiently. 'Of course we can. This could be a matter of life and death for the poor creature!'

'Please don't tell my mum!' Overhearing the latest order, Daniel emerged from the storeroom. His sudden appearance made Pandora jump and the chubby little dog started to yap, while Adam Hope tried to stop her from jumping off the high bench.

'Don't tell your mum what?' A new voice could be heard from outside in the corridor. It was Mrs Winterton herself. She came into the lab, dressed in a smart, dark blue, sleeveless evening-dress. 'Daniel, what have you been up to?'

Pandora's yapping bark had brought Mr Browning striding down the corridor. 'Is that a dog in the building?' he demanded irritably.

'I can't find a thing wrong with Pandora,' Adam Hope tried to tell Mrs Ponsonby, hanging on to the squirming, yapping dog above all the noise.

Mrs Ponsonby bossed and tutted and Daniel began to cry, while Mrs Winterton stood silently amid the chaos. Mandy and James got slowly to their feet and brushed themselves down, dreading what would happen next.

'Things can't get any worse,' James muttered, gazing at Honey's empty cage.

'Want to bet?' Mandy nudged him to make him look towards the door.

And there stood Joanna Davey, half hidden by the caretaker's broad figure. There was no mistaking her bright orange fleece and her neat, shiny dark hair. She looked as if she'd just come in from the cold. Her face was fresh and rosy, her jacket zipped up to the chin.

'Hi, Emily!' she said, smiling at the confusion, thinking that noisy Pandora and Mrs Ponsonby had caused it all. She stepped past Mr Browning and squeezed into the lab.

Mandy stared, then backed away. For one mad moment, she thought that if she stood in front of Honey's empty cage, she would be able to keep the hamster's disappearance secret from her owner.

Joanna unzipped her jacket. 'I came to see the second half of the show,' she told them briskly. 'John said he didn't mind staying at home to babysit Mabel's new litter. We thought . . . it was a shame to waste . . . both the tickets we'd bought . . .' Her voice slowed to a halt as she looked from Emily to Adam Hope, to Mandy's startled grandparents, then to Mrs Ponsonby and Pandora.

'Er-hum!' James joined Mandy in front of the shelf. He coughed and shuffled noisily.

'Never mind "er-hum"!' Mrs Ponsonby broke the awkward silence. She bustled forward to take Joanna's hand. 'I'm Amelia Ponsonby from

Bleakfell Hall. You've probably heard my name in the village.'

The newcomer looked blankly at her.

'The fact is, my dear, we have some bad news. Come and sit on this stool and compose yourself. Are you ready?'

Mandy watched the clouds gather on Joanna Davey's clear, bright face.

'I'm afraid that your little hamster, Honey, has got out of her cage and run away! But don't worry, we'll send out search parties throughout the school,' Mrs Ponsonby assured her. 'We'll comb the building from top to bottom. We'll send people out into the grounds to look. With Amelia Ponsonby in charge, we won't leave a stone unturned!'

Nine

'No! Definitely no!' Mandy's gran stood up to Mrs Ponsonby. 'We can't cancel everything just to find one missing hamster!'

A bell had sounded to signal the end of the interval. The audience was filing back into the hall. In the biology lab, the debate over Honey was fierce.

'It may be just one insignificant small creature to you, Dorothy Hope,' Mrs Ponsonby challenged, 'but to poor Joanna, this hamster is a beloved member of her family!'

James grimaced at Mandy. Even he thought

this was going a bit too far.

'I agree with Dorothy,' Mandy's grandad interrupted. 'The show must go on!'

'Think of all the effort that's gone into this Christmas show,' Adam Hope reminded everyone. He gave Mandy an apologetic glance. 'Sorry, love, I'm on your gran's side. Mrs Winterton has put in weeks of rehearsal, all the kids in the show have given up their free time, and there are hundreds of people in the audience all looking forward to the second half.'

Mandy bit her lip and nodded. But what about Honey? She made rapid calculations about how she and James might be able to continue the search, even if the show did go on.

Meanwhile, the red pom-pom on Mrs Ponsonby's velvet beret was trembling with indignation. She still seemed determined to call a halt to the show. 'I'm surprised at you, Adam! As a vet, I would have thought your first priority would be to help any animal in trouble!'

'Stop!' At last Joanna Davey spoke out. She stood up and went towards Mrs Ponsonby. 'Thank you,' she said quietly. 'Of course I'm upset about Honey, but really, there's no question of stopping the show to look for her.'

'My dear!' Mrs Ponsonby was about to dismiss her point of view. 'I know you're trying to be brave, but—'

'It's OK, we can do both,' Mandy cut in. Time was getting short. A second bell had rung to call the audience to their seats. 'We can look for Honey *and* carry on with the show!'

Mrs Ponsonby glared at her, then suddenly changed her mind. 'Exactly! This is what I've been saying all along,' she blustered. 'It's a question of organisation. Joanna, Emily, Adam – you and I will continue to lead the search operation from here in the biology lab. Mrs Winterton, dear, you must go back to your orchestra. And Mandy and James, it's time for you to run along and take your places backstage!'

Mandy frowned. But there was no time to argue. For the time being, they must leave it to the grown-ups.

A final bell announced the end of the interval and the start of the second half of the show.

'What about Daniel?' James asked, as he and Mandy dashed along the corridor. Mrs Ponsonby had overlooked the very person who was responsible for the hamster's disappearance.

Mandy shrugged and headed for her stage-left entrance. She pulled the wide brim of her witch's hat firmly down and prepared to go on stage. 'I don't know. I just wish there was a magic spell to get rid of Mrs Ponsonby!'

James grinned. 'You don't trust her to find Honey?'

'No way!' Mandy pictured the chaos that Amelia Ponsonby and Pandora might cause. 'If I was a hamster in hiding and I saw that red pom-pom and ball of yapping cream fur heading towards me, I'd run a mile!'

Mandy's part in the second half of the show was smaller than in the first. She had a scene with the Little Mermaid's seven sisters, where they pleaded with her to save the mermaid and bring her back to the sea. There was more mixing of magic potions, more hissing and cackling, before she sent the sisters off on their mercy mission. After that, she was free until the finale.

Mandy went through her speeches without a flicker of stage fright. Confidently she whirled her cloak and clawed at the sisters with her long fingernails. She threw foam-rubber toads into her boiling cauldron with gay abandon. One last screech, and she was gone.

Off-stage almost before she knew it, she had at least half an hour before she was needed again.

Now! she said to herself. *Now for the serious business of finding Honey.*

First she had to find out how far the grown-ups had got, but she hoped to do this without crossing Mrs Ponsonby's path. Since she was probably still in the lab organising the others, Mandy decided to try the home economics room and other nooks and crannies along the ground-floor corridor.

She found her grandparents amongst the cookery books and cake tins. 'Any luck?'

They shook their heads.

'If Amelia Ponsonby calls me "Dorothy, dear" once more, I'll . . . I'll . . . !'

'Explode,' Mandy's grandad concluded. He lifted the lid of a round tin and looked inside. 'Sorry we missed your second half,' he told Mandy.

'That's OK. Have you seen James lately?' She knew that he too had a gap before he was needed onstage for his final scene.

Her grandad nodded. 'Heading that-a-way with little Daniel.' He pointed down the empty corridor towards the lockers.

Mandy scooted off, turning right into the cloakroom, and found both James and Daniel Winterton scouring the area.

Hearing her footsteps, James glanced round. 'We think Honey managed to nip out of the lab,' he told her.

'How do you know?' Quickly Mandy began to test the locker doors and peer inside those that opened.

'We don't know for sure. But it turns out that Daniel's bag of crisps was crushed and had a hole in it. He left a little trail of crumbs out in the corridor. Our hunch is that Honey might have followed it.' James went on looking.

Once more Mandy had the panicky thought that the school was big and the hamster very small. She jerked open more locker doors. Stepping sideways, she heard a crunch underfoot. She looked down and saw that she'd trodden on a crisp. As she stooped to brush it off the sole of her black pointed shoe, she glanced under the row of lockers.

'Oh!' She gasped, then froze. 'H-H-Honey!'

A tiny, furry face stared back from the shallow gap. White whiskers twitched, black eyes glinted.

Behind her, James and Daniel crept to look. Three pairs of human eyes stared at one beady black pair of hamster eyes. Three huge faces pressed against the polished floor, gazing at one sweet, honey-coloured hamster.

'Here, Honey!' Mandy breathed.

The hamster retreated further under the lockers.

'Try reaching her!' James muttered.

Gingerly Mandy slid her fingers into the gap.

Honey shuffled backwards against the wall.

'Careful!' James warned.

Mandy stretched her arm and hand until her fingertips touched something soft and furry. 'Nearly!'

Daniel said nothing. He held his breath and peered into the cranny.

Mandy's fingers closed round a warm, small body. So, so near! 'Ouch!'

The hamster had bitten her. She clambered over Mandy's hand out of reach.

'She's getting away again!' Daniel cried.

'Which way?' Mandy couldn't see what was happening.

'This way!' James crawled towards the boys' cloakroom door. 'No, that way!' He changed direction and headed towards the girls' room.

Getting to her feet, Mandy tripped on her cloak and stumbled over Daniel. James had crawled as far as the doorway into the girls' cloakroom and was pointing through a narrow gap.

'She ran in there!' he hissed.

Mandy opened the door and followed the

hamster, shivering as icy air from an open window hit her. The tiled floor was freezing cold. There were a dozen cubicles with gaps under the doors, a radiator and a wastepaper bin at the far end, and above that the window to the outside world.

It wasn't hard for Mandy to spot where Honey was headed. The hamster's cream fur showed up plainly against the dark terracotta tiles as she scuttled down the aisle between the cubicles and leaped for the waste bin, clinging to its wire sides and hauling herself up.

For a few vital seconds Mandy hesitated. Should she make a grab for Honey and risk knocking her off the bin?

'Get her, Mandy!' James peered in through the door. 'Quick, before she reaches the window-sill!'

She did as he said, but not soon enough.

Honey had scrambled up from the bin to the sill, her back legs dangling dangerously until she hauled herself to safety. Her feet slid across the polished tiled surface, sending her skidding towards the edge again. Then she regained her footing and headed for the open window.

'Now!' James urged. Honey's front legs were already reaching for the stone sill outside the window. Her rear end was tipping upwards and hopping over the ledge.

Mandy made a rapid lunge and the hamster gave a quick flick of her squat hind legs. She was gone – out of sight through the gap in the window, into the dark, cold night.

'Now she'll die!' Daniel's voice was hollow with shock. 'She'll freeze to death!'

'Not if we can help it!' James was already heading for the nearest door out into the school grounds, followed by Mandy and Daniel. But even he wasn't prepared for what greeted them when they stepped outside.

'It's snowing!' Mandy gasped.

Huge snowflakes drifted from the black sky and settled on the path. There was a thin covering on the parked cars, the grass verges, the row of holly trees beyond. Yet the sky had been clear when they'd driven across in the early evening, and no snow had been forecast.

'At least it means we'll be able to see footprints!' James ran on. He picked out the cloakroom window through which Honey had escaped and stopped below it.

Mandy stepped out into the snow with a shiver. 'Come on, we can't let Honey down now!' she urged Daniel. 'Think of what Norvik would have done! He would have braved the freezing cold and saved everyone in the castle!'

The little boy nodded. His head went up, his shoulders back, as he followed Mandy out into the cold.

'Can you see anything?' She took Daniel with her down the sloping path to join James. There were bushes at the foot of the cloakroom window into which the hamster could have jumped.

James put out his arms to hold the others back. 'Don't tread anywhere near where she landed,' he warned. 'We need to be able to see the footprints.'

'But the snow's covering them up fast.' Mandy crouched down to find a clue. Soft white flakes landed swiftly and silently. In the dim glow cast by the cloakroom light across the shadowy ground, it was difficult to see anything as small as the prints left by a tiny hamster.

'Over here!' Daniel called. He'd stayed on the path, where the light from a lamp in the carpark was brighter, and was now pointing to scuff-marks in the snow.

Mandy and James hurried over. The marks had definitely been made by a tiny animal with sharp claws.

'They're heading this way!' Mandy took up the trail, pointing to a gap between two parked cars. 'No, I've lost them!' she sighed. The tracks had petered out beside one of the cars.

'No, look!' Daniel found them again. He picked up the trail across the car's snow-covered bonnet; tiny footprints leading towards an overhanging holly tree. The track ended at the very edge of the bonnet.

'Is it my imagination, or is the bottom branch on that tree moving?' James said quietly.

Mandy followed the direction of his pointing finger. Sure enough, the slim branch of dark green, prickly leaves swayed and dipped in the lamplight. She had a glimpse of bright red berries as the twig moved again, a flurry of falling snow, and a fleeting glance of a small, pale animal scuttling for cover amongst the leaves.

Lifting her face, Mandy stared up at the tall, dark tree. 'Honey's hiding in the holly!' she whispered to James and Daniel, feeling the freezing touch of the softly falling snow.

Ten

'Go and fetch my mum and dad!' Mandy kept
her eye fixed on the small, shivering shape of
Honey the hamster. 'Go on, Daniel! Bring them
here as quick as you can!'

As the little boy stopped hesitating and ran
off, she confided her main fear to James.
'Hamsters hate the cold. They belong in warm
deserts, not countries where it snows. Daniel
was right: Honey will die if she stays out here
for much longer!'

James stared at the prickly branches of the
holly tree as the hamster climbed quickly out

of reach. 'I could try to bring her down,' he suggested.

'She wouldn't let you get near.' Judging by recent experience, the little runaway was determined not to be caught. 'You'd only scare her, and she'd probably give us the slip. Then we'd be back where we started.'

'So we wait for your mum and dad?' James craned his neck and gazed anxiously into the tangle of evergreen leaves, at the spot where Honey now squatted in the angle formed between a branch and the main trunk of the five-metre-high tree. 'Will they know what to do?'

'I hope so.' Mandy crept nearer to the tree, relieved to see that at least the holly leaves sheltered Honey from the snow. But the hamster sat hunched and unhappy, her dark eyes blinking down at Mandy, and her eyelids slowly beginning to close. 'James, she seems to be going to sleep up there!'

'Oh no! We mustn't let her!' He pushed forward to join Mandy. 'You know what that would mean?'

Honey huddled against the trunk, eyelids drooping.

'What?' Mandy kept her voice low, predicting the answer James would give.

'That she's drifting into unconsciousness because of the cold – hypothermia!' he whispered back.

Mandy knew from her parents that this was where the body temperature dropped so low that an animal or person could no longer stay awake. Once they lost consciousness, it was usually the end. 'You're right. We can't let her fall asleep!' she decided. Now there was no longer time to wait for her mum and dad. Instead, she began to hitch up her long black skirt, ready to climb.

'You'll get scratched to bits!' James stepped in front and took her place.

'But I've got my cloak!' Mandy insisted. And we have to wrap Honey in something warm as soon as we reach her!' She set her foot on the bottom branch, feeling more snow slide from the leaves as she put her weight on it and hauled herself off the ground.

Pushing up between the branches, Mandy felt a hundred sharp pinpricks on her bare arms and legs. Still out of reach on her overhead perch, Honey scarcely moved. Her eyes blinked once, twice, three times. Then they stayed shut.

'Too late!' James breathed. He saw the hamster sway unsteadily on the branch.

Mandy chose another foothold and climbed again. This time, she could almost reach out with her fingertips and touch Honey. But not quite.

'Mandy, she's unconscious!' James had given up hope. 'Any second now, she's going to fall!'

The leaves scratched at her skin and pulled at her clothes, but Mandy climbed to the next branch. And now she could reach. With trembling hands she stretched across. Her fingers closed around the hamster's shivering body and she plucked her from the tree.

Honey's eyes flickered open as Mandy balanced on her branch and cradled her. Swiftly Mandy eased the cloak from her shoulders to wrap it around the trembling creature.

'Is she still alive?' James called anxiously from below.

'Yes!' Only just. Mandy knew hypothermia made a patient sleepy and confused. You had to keep them warm, try to make them stay awake. Gently, still balancing precariously, she began to rub the hamster's fur with her cloak.

'Here comes Daniel with your mum and dad!' James called. He turned and called them. 'Mr and Mrs Hope, over here!'

Mandy heard a burst of loud music from inside the school as doors opened and help arrived. 'James, I'm stuck!' she hissed. With both hands cradling Honey in the bulky black cloak, how on earth was she going to climb back down to the ground?

'You two go and help Mandy. I'll fetch a blanket and stuff from the Land-rover.' Emily Hope spoke quickly to Mandy's dad and Daniel.

'Bring the spare infra-red lamp that we brought with us from the Daveys' house!' Adam Hope called after her. He ran to James, closely followed by Daniel. They all stared up at Mandy and Honey.

'How is she?' Daniel called in his high, tense voice.

'Still conscious!' Mandy rubbed and massaged the tiny body. Honey's black eyes blinked, her round ears and long whiskers twitched. She was so busy concentrating on keeping the hamster alive that she forgot where she was.

'Whoa, Mandy. Watch out!' her dad called up as she swayed and almost fell.

Mandy wobbled and jolted back against the trunk. She glanced dizzily at the ground.

'Sit down!' Adam Hope instructed. 'When your mum brings a blanket, I'll send James up on to the branch below you, then Daniel, then me. We'll form a human chain for you to pass the hamster from one to another. Mandy, did you hear that?'

'Yes.' She held her breath, stroking and rubbing the weak creature cradled in her hands.

'Right, we're ready!' Her dad took the blanket from Emily Hope, handed it to James and sent the two boys up the tree.

The whole tree shook with their weight. Mandy held tight to Honey.

'OK, Mandy!' James climbed until he was within reach. He passed the thick red dog-blanket to her. 'Wrap Honey up and hand her to me!'

Carefully, without letting the cold air get to her again, Mandy followed instructions. Soon she had the hamster safely snuggled inside the blanket.

'Easy does it!' Mr Hope instructed from below. 'That's right; James has got her. Now, Daniel, you get ready.'

Slowly, smoothly, the hamster was handed from Mandy to James, from James to Daniel, and finally from Daniel to Mr Hope, standing with two feet firmly planted on the snowy ground.

'Now come down as quickly as you can,' Emily Hope told them, as Mandy's dad took the lamp, turned and headed indoors with the tiny patient.

Mandy looked down, her head spinning. 'How did I get up here in the first place?' She couldn't remember which branches she'd used or how she'd made her way up through the spiky leaves.

The headlights of a car just driving in through the gates helped her. The lights shone on the holly tree as Daniel, then James, then Mandy slowly made their way to safety. They stayed on, catching the children in a bright spotlight, as the car door opened and closed, and a tall figure came hurrying across the snowy carpark.

'Daniel?' The man sounded puzzled as he drew near. 'Is that you?'

He stopped short of Mandy's snow-covered, bedraggled group, the collar of his padded jacket turned up, half hiding his face.

Mandy saw Daniel's eyes widen and his mouth fall open. He gasped and turned to the stranger. Then he was running away from the holly tree, up the path in the direct line of the headlight beam, kicking up loose snow as he sprinted across the carpark.

The man spread his arms wide to catch him.

'Dad!' Daniel sprang at him and was lifted off his feet and swung round. 'You're back!'

Mr Winterton laughed and landed him safely on the ground. 'I set off home early as a surprise, to see Mum's show. Then I got held up on the motorway. But here I am, and not too late, I hope!' He hugged his son then held his hand tight.

Emily Hope grinned at James and Mandy, urging them up the slope. 'Happy Christmas!' she said to Daniel's father. 'You're just in time for the finale!'

Eleven

'Go and take your bow!' Emily Hope insisted.

The last song had been sung, the final curtain had come down and the audience was beginning to clap as actors, dancers and musicians came back on stage.

'But Mum, we need to find out how Honey is!' All Mandy wanted to do was to dash along the corridor to the biology lab to se the patient.

Mrs Hope held firm. 'Leave that to us. Don't let Mrs Winterton down. Go along.'

So Mandy unhitched her snow-covered skirt and flung her cloak back round her shoulders.

She rammed her bent hat down on her head and stomped off down the corridor. 'I will if you will,' she muttered to James.

He nodded, and they split off from Daniel and Mr Winterton to head for the stage, just in time for James to take his bow with the rest of the prince's courtiers.

As she stood in the dark wings, waiting for her turn, Mandy felt the snow on her hat and wig begin to melt. Water dribbled down her forehead and dripped off the end of her nose. Her feet squelched in her pointed shoes.

'Go on, Mandy!' Susan Collins urged as the witch music played.

Squelch-squelch-squelch! Mandy dripped and dribbled on to the stage under the hot overhead lights. When she bent her head to take her bow, the last chunks of melting snow slid from the brim and landed in a wet puddle at her feet.

The audience cheered. A sea of hands clapped. At the back of the hall, she caught sight of her grandparents standing by the door, smiling proudly.

'Easy!' Mandy whispered to Susan, who came on last of all to take her bow. 'There's nothing to this acting stuff!'

Susan grinned. 'Says you!' She bowed and lapped up the applause. In the front row, her mother and father stood and cheered.

Then the lights dimmed and the curtain came down for the very last time.

'That's the best Christmas show the school has ever put on!' Mandy overheard the head teacher, Mr Wakeham, congratulating Mrs Winterton as she and James dashed off stage. 'Really excellent. A credit to us all!'

'I wonder if Mrs Winterton knows that Mr Winterton is here?' James ran along the ground-floor corridor to keep up with Mandy.

Mandy had gathered her long, damp skirt round her knees and was sprinting to find out the latest news about Honey. Her arms and legs were smarting from dozens of tiny scratches made by the holly leaves and her shoes still squelched with every step.

'Hey!' Mr Browning saw from a distance the mess she was making of his nice polished floor.

They ignored him and sped towards the lab.

Mandy burst through the door first. Her mum and dad, Joanna Davey, Daniel and Mr Winterton and, last but not least, Mrs Ponsonby and Pandora, were crowded round the three hamster cages on the shelf. All were looking anxiously at the cage with the special lamp clipped to the wire-mesh front, carefully angled to direct heat inside.

Mandy and James came to a halt. Adam Hope was still at work, carefully watching the effect of the infra-red lamp on his patient. It seemed that everyone was holding their breath.

Slowly they went to join the group. Breaking the silence, they heard the squeak of Henry's exercise wheel and saw that the school hamster hadn't been put off his stride by the large group of spectators round his cage. He trod steadily, putting in his nightly run.

And Mandy noticed that Marmalade too had ignored the crisis. The bright cinnamon hamster was sitting on his haunches at the front of his cage, quietly licking his paws and using them to groom his fat cheeks and round, hairy ears. When he saw Mandy and James join the group of anxious onlookers, he cocked his head to one side, as if to ask, 'Why all the fuss?'

'Well?' Joanna Davey said at last. She moved towards Adam Hope and let James and Mandy have their first glimpse of Honey's cage.

The patient sat hunched up, a little round

ball of silky cream fur, her head pulled in towards her chest, her black eyes closed.

Her pulse and temperature are back to normal,' Mandy's dad reported. 'The infra-red seems to have done the trick. This hamster is going to be just fine!'

'Of course, if it hadn't been for Pandora, the whole story would have had an unhappy ending!' Mrs Ponsonby announced to anyone who would listen.

Joanna Davey had thanked Adam and Emily Hope and was making her way towards Mandy and James, her face all smiles.

'How do you make that out?' Mandy's grandad asked. He and Dorothy had come straight from the hall, down the crowded corridor and back to the lab. 'What did Pandora do – pick up the hamster's scent?'

The mistress of Bleakfell Hall waved him away impatiently. 'It stands to reason: if poor Pandora hadn't been feeling unwell, I would never have brought her in here to see Adam. And if I hadn't been here to organise the search party . . . well, goodness knows what would have happened!'

Emily Hope caught Mandy's eye and grinned. Her dad winked at her.

'Of course, Mandy, James and Daniel did play their small part!' Mrs Ponsonby conceded. She tucked Pandora more firmly under her plump arm.

'Well, thank you, everyone!' Honey's relieved owner smiled again. She turned specially to Daniel, who was still holding his father's hand.

The little boy blushed and dropped his gaze to stare at his trainers. Perhaps he'd looked over Joanna's shoulder and seen his mother come into the room.

Mrs Winterton looked flushed and tired. For a moment, after she'd closed the door, she sank against it and closed her eyes. The evening had obviously been a big strain.

Everyone fell silent and turned to watch her open her eyes. She took in Mandy and James in their bedraggled costumes and the knot of grown-ups by the hamsters' cages. Then she saw Daniel hanging tightly on to the hand of a tall, fair-haired figure. 'Mark!'

Mr Winterton grinned and held on to Daniel. Together they went across the room. 'Happy

Christmas, Karen!' he murmured, kissing her cheek.

'And well done, Mrs Winterton!' Dorothy Hope chimed in. She began to applaud the music teacher for the superb show which she'd just put on.

'Yes, brilliant!' Mandy's grandad agreed. 'Wonderful music!'

Mark Winterton put his arm around his wife's waist. Soon everyone in the room had joined in the applause.

'What happened to Honey?' Mrs Winterton blushed, suddenly remembering the missing hamster.

'*Da-dah!*' Mandy stepped forward to show her that the runaway was safely back. She grinned at Daniel. 'She had an adventure in a holly tree, but Daniel helped to save her—'

'Er-hum!' Mrs Ponsonby made a loud, throat-clearing noise.

'*And* Pandora,' Mandy added, with a quick, secret smile in James's direction. 'Without Pandora, none of this would have worked out right!'

'Let's get this straight. This is *not* a Christmas

present!' Mark and Karen Winterton had driven over to Animal Ark with Daniel. It was a week and a half after Christmas. The cards were still hanging from the beams in the Animal Ark kitchen; the Christmas tree still glistened in the corner of the sitting-room.

'We don't believe in buying animals as Christmas presents,' Mrs Winterton explained. She was dressed in a bright blue jacket with a red tartan scarf tied round her neck, looking relaxed and happy now the strain of producing the school show was over.

'Good.' Adam Hope nodded. 'So, Daniel, this is an *un*-Christmas present!'

The little boy stood in the kitchen doorway, his dark eyes shining. 'Can Mandy and James come and help me choose?'

'Try and stop us!' James jumped up from his seat. He and Mandy had been working at morning surgery, helping Jean to keep things running smoothly in Reception. They'd just come across to the house for lunch.

'Is that OK?' Mandy asked her mum.

'Just let me get this straight.' Emily Hope took off her white coat and hung it on a hook behind the door. She eased her long hair out of its ponytail, then turned to Karen Winterton. 'You've changed your mind. You're saying that Daniel can keep a pet hamster after all?'

The teacher put an arm around her son's shoulder. 'Daniel has been showing us how responsible he can be,' she told them. 'Every day this holiday, he's visited Lilac Cottage to help clean out Honey and Marmalade's cages. And Mark's convinced me that Daniel deserves another chance.'

'And I only have to work away from home for another six weeks,' Mr Winterton continued. 'After that I'll be back for good. I can help Daniel to look after his hamster.'

'He'll be able to bring the baby home in about a fortnight's time. It'll be company for him while his dad's away again,' Mrs Winterton explained.

Mandy had watched the glow on the little boy's face as he gazed from his mum to his dad and back again. Now she grabbed her jacket. 'Where are you going to get your un-Christmas present from?' She imagined driving over to Walton with the Wintertons to visit the pet shop there.

'From here in Welford,' Mark Winterton put

in. 'Daniel specially wanted you and James to help him choose.'

'Whereabouts in Welford?' James too was curious as he, Mandy and the Wintertons said goodbye to Adam and Emily Hope and got into the car.

Mandy gave her mum and dad a wave as they pulled out into the lane under the wooden Animal Ark sign. It was a clear, bright day. Almost-melted snow lay banked against the walls and in the hollows of the fields.

'At Joanna Davey's house.' Mrs Winterton put the final piece into place. 'You know that one of her hamsters had babies recently?'

Mandy laughed and said yes, she did. Mabel's six youngsters had all survived their difficult birth. The Daveys had taken good care of them. Meanwhile, Tom and Dorothy Hope had given the Daveys their promised breathing-space and taken Honey and Marmalade home to Lilac Cottage on the night of the school play, as planned. Now the babies were all doing well, and Honey and Marmalade were back with the Daveys.

'Great! We get to see Honey again!' James grinned.

Welford village was in sight. They passed the Fox and Goose, the church, the post office.

'Hello, everyone!' Joanna Davey was waiting on her front doorstep to greet them. She showed them into the house and straight through to the living-room, where she now kept all three pet hamsters. 'All fit and well!' she reported, waving first towards Marmalade and Honey's cages, then towards the large nursery-cage where Mabel was looking after her young ones.

Mandy took a quick look at Marmalade, then Honey. Both hamsters hopped cheekily to the front of their cages and twitched their noses.

'It's as if she never had an adventure in a holly tree!' James murmured. The cream hamster's cheek pouches were stuffed with food; her dark eyes were bright and shiny.

Daniel had gone ahead to look at Mabel and her babies. 'Oh!' he gasped.

So Mandy and James went to look too.

There, in a nest of soft blue rags and wood shavings, rested the white hamster and her two-week-old litter. She was lying on her side, letting them feed. They snuggled against her, six babies with a fine covering of silky hair, and tiny round ears laid flat against their heads.

Daniel peered in and sighed.

'Choose one!' his dad instructed.

'Which?' Daniel glanced over his shoulder to ask James and Mandy.

'You decide!' they insisted.

He looked up and down the row of tightly snuggled youngsters. He chose one, then another, changing his mind until he'd gone along the whole row and was about to start again.

In the background, Joanna smiled at Mr and Mrs Winterton.

'That one . . . no, that one!' Daniel continued.

Then one baby made up Daniel's mind for him. It was a pale fawn hamster. As it finished feeding it broke away from the group and bravely approached the front of the cage, clutching at the bars with its tiny pink paws. It stared boldly at Daniel with its ruby-red eyes.

'This one!' Daniel breathed.

'And what will you call it?' His dad crouched down beside him to look.

Daniel smiled happily. 'Norvik the Second,' he said without a second's hesitation. 'And Dad, you know what? This is the best *un*-Christmas present ever!'

Animal Ark series

Plus:
Little Animal Ark
Animal Ark Pets
Animal Ark Hauntings
Animal Ark Holiday Specials

Animal Ark™

**For more information about
Animal Ark and for the latest news
on the books and how you can
get involved, visit the website:**

www.animalark.co.uk

Hodder
Children's
Books

A division of Hachette Children's Books